DEKOK AND MURDER ON THE MENU

Books by A.C. Baantjer:

DeKok
and
Murder on the Menu

by

BAANTJER

translated from the Dutch by H.G. Smittenaar

NEW AMSTERDAM PUBLISHING, Inc.

ISBN 1 881164 31 4

Printing History:
 1st Dutch printing: April, 1990
 2nd Dutch printing: May, 1990
 3rd Dutch printing: June, 1990
 4th Dutch printing: July, 1990
 5th Dutch printing: October, 1990
 6th Dutch printing: November, 1990
 7th Dutch printing: February, 1991
 8th Dutch printing: February, 1991
 9th Dutch printing: July, 1991

1st American edition: 1992

Cover Design: Studio Combo (Netherlands)
Cover Photo: Maron Olthoff
Typography: Monica S. Rozier

DeKok
and
Murder on the Menu

1

Inspector DeKok, assigned to the ancient police station in the Warmoesstraat, Amsterdam, leaned comfortably back in his chair and looked, with a genial smile on his lips, at the young man who had placed himself on the chair next to his desk. Briefly, he scratched his nose and then stretched an index finger toward his visitor.

"What's your name?" he asked pleasantly.

"Jan ... Jan Schouten."

DeKok moved his lower lip forward: "A nice name ... Jan Schouten. Historical name. There was a famous admiral by that name. And how old are you?"

"Seventeen. I am from Rotterdam. My father owns a large book store there."

"And you want to become a police detective?"

The young man nodded emphatically. "I always read the books Baantjer writes about you. I think they are great. Real thrillers. I would love to get involved in a murder with you and Vledder ... totally ... from beginning to end. I think that would be awesome."

DeKok grinned. "I am sorry, but that's impossible. Anyway ... if I were you I wouldn't be so quick to believe everything that Baantjer writes about me. I know him, you know. I like him. We visit from time to time and I tell him about the sort of things that happen to a police-detective in Amsterdam. Baantjer, however, has the tendency to present the facts in a much more complicated and romantic way than they really are. He embellishes a lot. Writers call that poetic license, but in my opinion it is just cheating."

Deep creases appeared in the forehead of Jan Schouten.

"You mean your work is not difficult and thrilling?" His voice sounded somewhat disappointed.

DeKok laughed at the boy's perplexed face. "Sometimes," he said slowly, "sometimes it is very complex and maybe even thrilling. As far as that goes, Baantjer is right. I won't deny it. But sometimes, for instance when I stand waiting in a ground-soaking rain for somebody that I am not even sure is going to show up, then those are the times that I wish I'd chosen a different profession. Bookseller, for instance."

Jan Schouten snorted. "That's no prize, either," he said, sadly. "I know from looking at my parents. A lot of headaches, long days ... My grandfather started the business before the war. Now my father is carrying on and I am supposed to be the third Schouten to continue the tradition."

DeKok nodded. "It seems a reasonable wish on your father's part. Like father, like son. It wasn't too long ago that it was the most common thing in the world."

Jan shook his head. "I look at my father and see the worries, the penny-pinching ..." He did not complete the sentence. "That busy book shop, frankly, is not something I look forward to." The young man laughed. "I told you, I want to be a police detective."

Reassuringly DeKok leaned forward: "I'd sleep on it, if I were you. For a while, anyway. If you then still ..." He stopped and, over the head of his visitor, looked at his assistant, Vledder, who rushed into the office in a high state of excitement.

"Come and look," he yelled.

"Where?"

"The loading dock, in the back."

"What's there?"

Vledder motioned, impatiently.

"Just come along."

Sighing, DeKok rose. He placed his hand on the head of young Schouten. "Just wait here a minute. I'll be right back." Then he shuffled after Vledder, out of the detective room and through the long corridor.

They descended two sets of stairs and crossed the building to the rear entrance. Vledder opened the door to the loading dock and pointed to the parking area.

"Look ... a new Volkswagen Golf."

DeKok looked at him, mystified.

"So what?"

"That's ours!"

"What!?"

Eyes bright and excited, Vledder nodded.

"Our old Beetle is going to the junk yard," he shouted enthusiastically. "I think that the higher-ups finally realized the mortal danger involved in driving that old rattle-trap. It's an insult to the police. People laugh at us when we arrive in that rust bucket."

DeKok did not react. He chewed his lower lip and his wide face looked somber. "Junk yard." It sounded melancholy.

Insensitive, Vledder looked at him. "Yes, junk yard. In case you didn't know, that's where they take old cars."

DeKok walked away and strolled, past the gleaming Golf, toward the old, dented Beetle. With a tender gesture he placed his hand on the roof.

Vledder joined him and invitingly opened the door of the new Golf.

"Don't you want to see how it fits?"

DeKok shook his head. His hand remained on the roof of the old Beetle. With a tremor in his voice he said softly: "Junk yard! It didn't deserve that."

Vledder reacted with amazement. "What do you want ... preserve it ... conserve it ... put it in a museum ... with a sign ... In this drove inspectors DeKok and Vledder ... defying death?" His voice dripped with sarcasm.

Resignedly DeKok shrugged his shoulders.

"I was used to that old bucket ... I loved it. Always ready to go. I even loved its dents and scratches. We spent a great many hours in it and, as far back as I can remember, it never left us in the lurch. That ...eh, that forms a bond."

Vledder grinned. "You sentimental old fool." Then, with a gesture of utter contempt, the young inspector kicked the flaking, rusting bumper. "This is a dead thing ... a used tool, that's all. A heap of old rust ... ready for the junk yard. What more do you want?"

DeKok did not answer. He took his hand away and, with bowed head, turned his back on the Beetle. Vledder followed him.

"Don't you want to try the Golf? Believe me, it is something else. Much more room and it drives like a dream. There's just no comparison between it and the old Beetle." The young inspector pleaded invitingly: "Come on, just sit behind the wheel a moment."

Determined, DeKok shook his head and continued on. At the door he turned and looked, for long seconds, at the old, discarded Volkswagen. A thoughtful look was on his face.

"Sometimes," he said softly, "I think that inanimate objects have souls as well. And maybe ... maybe I know for sure."

* * *

"Have I kept you waiting long?"

Jan Schouten looked at him, beaming. "No way," he said, cheerfully, "impossible to get bored in this room." He nodded in the direction of a man, being interrogated by an inspector, in another part of the room. "That's a real burglar," he whispered. "He's just been brought in by two constables. Caught in the act, they said."

Smiling, DeKok sat down and picked up the conversation where they had left off.

"I don't understand you ... You come all the way from Rotterdam to Amsterdam just to tell me that you want to be a police detective?" His voice sounded unbelieving. The boy shook his head.

"Father sent me."

DeKok showed surprise.

"Your father?"

The young man nodded. " 'This is really a case for Inspector DeKok,' he said. And because I was the one to find it, I was allowed to come to Amsterdam to bring it to you."

DeKok scowled.

"Do you always speak in riddles?"

Jan Schouten shook his head. "It's not a riddle and I don't speak in riddles." He changed his position. "Please give me a minute and I'll explain."

Resigned, DeKok nodded: "All the time you want."

Jan leaned a little forward: "We have a normal book shop. I mean ... father doesn't handle old, used, or antique books. It was just a coincidence."

"What?" asked DeKok. Jan Schouten made a soothing gesture.

"An old lady came into the shop, last week. My father knew her well. Her husband was already a client of grandfather. She told my father that her husband had passed away and she was planning to enter a rest home. In the rest home, however, there was no room for all the books that her husband had bought over the years, many from us. She asked if father was interested in the books, otherwise she would just give them to the junk man."

DeKok looked at him from half-closed eyes. "And ... father was interested?"

Young Schouten nodded: "We went together ... father and me. It was quite a collection. As the son of a book seller I am used to books, but, oh boy, the books in that house ... entire walls, filled to the ceiling. It took three trips to get everything to the warehouse."

"And then?" DeKok gestured impatiently.

Jan Schouten sighed.

"Father was busy in the store and not sure what to do with all those used books. I'm off from school. 'See if there is something there for the shop,' he said. So I went through the books we had picked up from Mrs. Donkersloot. And ... in an old history book ... I found this."

"What?" asked DeKok.

Jan unbuttoned his shirt and pulled out a rectangular piece of stiff paper which he handed to DeKok. "This," he said.

The old inspector looked at him suspiciously.

"This is a menu," he said, somewhat surprised. "A regular menu from the Hotel-Restaurant *De Poort van Eden* (Eden's Gate) in Amsterdam." He glanced a question at the young man. "What ... eh, what is peculiar about that?"

Jan Schouten pointed at the menu. "Please turn it over."

DeKok did as he was asked and on the back of the menu he discovered a spidery handwriting.

"I, Hendrik Peter Donkersloot," read the old inspector, "hereby confess to a murder I committed. On the night of the 19th of July at 11:45 PM I fired with my pistol, an old Sauer 7.6mm, with malice aforethought and with full knowledge of the consequences, a total of three shots at Frederik Ravenstein. He looked at me as if he'd seen a ghost, collapsed and was dead almost instantly. I was to meet him on the Westermarkt, behind the Wester Tower. It is a quiet spot. There I was to hand him 50,000 guilders, in bills of 100 guilders each. He was blackmailing me and because I knew there would be no end to his demands, I decided to kill him. At first I had planned to leave him there, but in order to delay the discovery of my deed, I dragged his body to the Prince's Canal and let it slip in the water. I am not sorry for what I did, but now, with the end in sight, I make this confession in order to prevent an innocent person from being charged with my crime."

DeKok glanced up. His face had become serious. "And this is what you found in an old history book?"

Jan nodded. "The menu stuck out a little and drew my attention. After I read the confession, I went to see father.

He said: 'It is an Amsterdam case, take it to Inspector DeKok in the Warmoesstraat'."

The gray haired detective thoughtfully rubbed his chin. "You didn't take it back to the old lady ... Mrs. Donkersloot?"

The boy shook his head. "I wanted to, but father said that it would be better to leave it with you."

DeKok smiled: "You have a wise father."

Jan pointed at the menu and asked: "Is it ... eh, is it real? Did this Hendrik Peter Donkersloot really commit murder?"

DeKok did not answer at once. For a while he stared thoughtfully into space.

"Last year, in July," he said, slowly, "the body of a man was found floating in the water of the Prince's Canal, behind the Wester Tower. His name was Frederik Ravenstein and there were three bullet holes in his chest."

2

Wide eyed, Jan Schouten looked at the gray-haired detective.

"So Hendrik Peter Donkersloot is a real murderer," he cried, surprised. "I can't believe it!"

"Why not?"

"I used to see him from time to time ... when he was still alive, of course ... in father's shop. He seemed a nice old man ... not a murderer."

DeKok looked at him, calculating. "What do murderers look like, according to you ... somebody with a big 'M' on his forehead?"

Jan shrugged his shoulders. "No idea. But not a nice old man like Mr. Donkersloot."

"Yet he confesses to murder ... a murder that has really been committed." DeKok pointed at the menu.

Jan Schouten pulled an agonized face.

"You are right. But I find it hard to believe." He looked a question at DeKok. "There's no possibility of a mistake?"

DeKok made an inviting gesture. "How? ... you tell me!"

The boy made a helpless gesture: "That ... eh, that I don't know ... not yet, but I want to think about it." He stood

up. "But if I remember anything, you'll hear from me."
DeKok rose as well.

"I'll wait for that, then," he said calmly. He shook the
young man's hand in farewell. "When you get home ... take
another look through those books in the collection. You're
on vacation anyway. Who knows ... maybe there are more
confessions."

* * *

After Jan Schouten had left, Vledder looked at DeKok
with surprise. "I know nothing about a body in the Prince's
Canal," he said.

Impassively, DeKok nodded to himself. "That was last
year when you where busy being lazy in the sun on the
Spanish coast."

Vledder ignored the remark. "Did you handle the case
at the time?"

DeKok shook his head. "The case was almost
immediately turned over to Narcotics. They held the
opinion, over there, that Frederik Ravenstein had become
the victim of a liquidation ... that he had been killed by
members of a rival gang. Frederik Ravenstein was known to
Narcotics for some time as a major drug dealer. Mainly
cocaine. They wanted to take over the case from us."

"Why?"

"They had hopes of discovering the supply lines during
the investigation, his connections ... connections with people
in South America."

Nodding, Vledder signified understanding.

DeKok chuckled: "That's what they were ... very
interested ... and enthusiastic. In passing they would quickly
solve the murder. Commissaris* Buitendam did not object

that the murder went to Narcotics. I was happy to be rid of the case. I had plenty to do at the time."

"And?"

"What do you mean?"

"Did they, in passing, solve the murder of Ravenstein?"

DeKok motioned toward the menu on his desk. "When I look at this confession, it seems they have been looking in the wrong direction. The murder of Frederik Ravenstein was not a liquidation by a rival gang, but the cold-blooded execution of a blackmailer."

Vledder grinned: "And the perpetrator is in the cemetery."

DeKok nodded slowly to himself. On his face was a thoughtful expression. "That's what it looks like."

Surprised, Vledder looked at him.

"That's what it looks like," he repeated, wondering, "You mean to say that Hendrik Peter Donkersloot is not dead and buried?"

Pushing his lower lip forward, DeKok pouted: "Probably, yes. But that's easy to check. A quick ring to the Rotterdam police and they'll figure that out for us."

Vledder wrinkled his forehead. "What are you thinking of?"

DeKok picked up the menu and looked again at the spidery handwriting.

"A cunning forgery."

* * *

They drove, from the Damrak, via Prins Hendrikkade and Haarlemmer Houttuinen, past the Haarlemmer Gate, across the Nassau Square to the Haarlemmer Road. A nebulous sun tried to penetrate an overcast sky. It was hot and sticky and the asphalt stank.

Beaming, Vledder looked aside.

"This is some difference from that old Beetle," he proclaimed enthusiastically. "It drives like a dream and it hugs the road a lot better." He tapped his colleague on the knee. "How are you?"

DeKok tightened the seat belt across his stomach.

"Is this necessary?"

Vledder nodded emphatically. "It's a law we can live with."

DeKok grumbled: "I feel like a horse ... in a harness."

Vledder ignored him. He turned the new Golf into to the Einstein Road and followed directions to The Hague.

"Shouldn't we have warned the guys in Narcotics that we're getting involved in their case?" Vledder asked.

DeKok shook his head. "That's not the way I see it. We're not getting involved in their case ... at least not for now. Only when I have a reasonable suspicion that Ravenstein's murder is not connected with drugs, but with blackmail ... then I'll ask Commissaris Buitendam if we can take the case back."

Vledder nodded understanding.

"Didn't Narcotics get anywhere ... in more than a year?"

DeKok shrugged his shoulders.

"I never heard anything from them ... no glowing reports, or positive news. I think that they've reached a dead end in their investigations."

"Then they could have returned the case?"

DeKok grinned: "And admit defeat?" The old inspector shook his head. "They'll never do that. Too proud. I think that they're waiting for new developments ... hope for a lucky break."

"They could have kept you informed."

DeKok spread both hands.

"It is also a little my own fault," he said soothing. "I never inquired regarding the state of affairs in the case. I wasn't that interested. I had other things to keep me occupied. It's only that this menu suddenly surfaces and the story intrigues me ..." He did not complete the sentence. With a grin he turned to his companion. "And I wanted you to have this little trip to Rotterdam ... in our new Golf."

Content, Vledder gripped the steering wheel a little tighter and pushed his foot a little harder on the gas.

* * *

Vledder glanced at DeKok. "You know where we have to go in Rotterdam? It is a difficult city to find anything. I've been here many times and I still get lost, every time."

DeKok groped in the breast pocket of his jacket for his notebook.

"People say the same things about Amsterdam," he growled. "And I have never been lost there." He smoothed out the wrinkled page of his notebook and looked at his scribbles. "According to Jan Schouten, the books were picked up from 1317 Mill Lane."

Vledder nodded. "I know how to find that," he announced excited. "That's not difficult. If I remember correctly it's a rather distinguished street in the Hillegersberg neighborhood."

DeKok stared out of the windshield. "I just hope she's still there," he said.

"Who?"

"Old Mrs. Donkersloot. Otherwise we'll have to ask bookseller Schouten if he knows to which rest home she has been banished."

Vledder laughed: "You call that banishment?"

DeKok nodded. "You know a better word?" he asked seriously.

The young inspector shrugged his shoulders. "It sounds so raw, so hard, so pitiless ... as if the ageing human, roughly and against his will, is banished from society and locked up until death." He frowned. "Surely it is not so bad to be cared for in a rest home."

DeKok pressed his lips together. "I am not interested in your opinion on the subject, or what definition you want to give it," his tone was short and stubborn. "I think banishment is the proper word in this connection and I stand by it."

Vledder looked at him, surprised. "A tender subject ... I think ... for you." DeKok did not react. He looked around at the maelstrom of Rotterdam traffic. He looked for comparisons with that of Amsterdam traffic, but recognized none.

Vledder slowed the Golf down and waved forward.

"And here is Mill Lane. You see, it even has trees."

DeKok nodded agreement.

Halfway down the street, Vledder parked the car along the side of the road. They got out and leisurely strolled the rest of the way.

Number 1317 turned out to be a fashionable brownstone with a gleaming, lacquered door and a small window at eye height behind a wrought iron grille. DeKok rang the bell. It took a while and then the little window opened and a wrinkled woman's face became visible behind the bars of the grille. A suspicious look was in the gray eyes.

DeKok produced his friendliest smile.

"Are you Mrs. Donkersloot?"

"Yes."

The old inspector performed a slight bow.

"My name is DeKok," his tone was friendly. "That's with ... eh, Kay-Oh-Kay." He pointed with his thumb. "And that's my colleague Vledder. We're police inspectors from the Warmoesstraat station in Amsterdam. We'd like to speak with you."

"What about?"

DeKok smiled again: "The subject is ... eh, too delicate to be discussed like this."

The woman hesitated a few seconds. Then her face disappeared and the gleaming, lacquered door was opened. In the opening stood a tall, thin woman in a dress of unrelieved black. Her hair was silver gray, pulled tightly along the sides of her face and ending in a chignon. The suspicious look remained in her eyes.

"Come in," she said, softly. "Please ignore the mess. I am in the process of taking everything out and sorting it for disposal." She closed the door behind the inspectors and shuffled ahead of them through a long, dark corridor. "In about a week I'll be going to a rest home. After my husband's death I tried for a few months to live here by myself, but it won't work. The house is too big, too old and too drafty."

The woman led the inspectors to a rather high-ceilinged room with four leather arm-chairs on a dull, bare parquet floor. She made an apologizing gesture. "It is not very cozy. But please sit down. The carpets have already been sold," she said.

DeKok lowered himself into one of the easy chairs and looked at an almost empty glass case.

"You have no help?" He sounded amazed.

21

Mrs. Donkersloot seated herself opposite him and shook her head.

"My husband and I have been living a retiring life for years. We didn't bother with anyone. We have no friends or acquaintances. I wouldn't know whom to ask for help."

"Had your husband been sick long?"

Mrs. Donkersloot shook her head. "Never anything wrong ... always as healthy as a horse." She gestured toward the empty chair. "One morning I woke up and that's where I found him ... dead. The doctor said it was a heart attack."

"Did your husband complain about chest pains?"

Mrs. Donkersloot shrugged her shoulders. "Not as far as I know. He never complained to me about it."

DeKok remained silent and then changed the subject: "According to my information your husband had an extensive library."

Mrs. Donkersloot nodded emphatically.

"His pride and joy." Briefly her eyes glistened. "Mostly history books and historical works. He was very interested in that. People should learn the lessons from history, he used to tell me. There are always periods in history which can be compared with today's events. History teaches us what the consequences were. It enables us to avoid the mistakes from the past."

DeKok bestowed an admiring smile: "That sounds profound."

The praise was visibly appreciated by Mrs. Donkersloot.

"My husband was a thinker ... a philosophical nature. He liked to reminisce about what he called 'The Pilgrimage of Mankind'."

DeKok leaned forward: "What ... eh, what did your husband do?"

22

"How do you mean?"

DeKok spread both hands. "Was he independently wealthy?" he asked.

Mrs. Donkersloot shook her head. "He was in business."

"That is a vague concept."

Mrs. Donkersloot glanced at the old sleuth. Briefly a smile lit up her face.

"That's what my husband business has always been for me ... vague."

"You weren't curious?"

Mrs. Donkersloot made a helpless gesture.

"Oh, in the beginning, of course." She gave him a tired smile. "Understandable. What woman is not interested in the comings and goings of her husband? But I always received such evasive and incomprehensible answers to my questions, that finally I did not ask him anything, any more ... about his business, I mean. Otherwise we conversed normally with each other. Hendrik liked that best."

DeKok nodded understanding.

"Did your husband ever go to Amsterdam for business?"

"Certainly. At least twice a month."

"For extended periods of time?"

Mrs. Donkersloot nodded.

"Two or three days at a time. Then he stayed overnight in Amsterdam."

DeKok looked at her intently.

"Where?"

"In the *De Poort van Eden* hotel."

---

* Commissaris: a rank equivalent to Captain.

3

Silently they drove away from Mill Lane in their new Golf. The busy Rotterdam traffic required all of Vledder's attention. A surly look was on the face of the young inspector. Next to him, hunched forward in the seat, hanging in his seat belt, was DeKok. In his mind he went once again over the interview with Mrs. Donkersloot. It surprised him that the woman had so easily accepted the visit from two Amsterdam police detectives. At no time had she asked for the real reason of the visit ... never asked what exactly was the object of their visit. And that, thus concluded DeKok, was very remarkable ... even unusual.

Had she been prepared? Had she expected that kind of visit ... how ... why? Was Mrs. Donkersloot really unaware of her husband's business ... or was it nonsense ... an excuse to avoid bothersome questions? A myriad of questions churned in his mind.

When they reached the thruway to Amsterdam and the traffic had become lighter, Vledder looked aside. "For that we had to drive all the way to Rotterdam?" he jeered.

Momentarily lost, DeKok looked at him. "What do you mean?"

Vledder snorted: "You didn't ask that Mrs. Donkersloot anything." Incomprehension resonated in his voice. "You didn't even discuss the murder in Amsterdam, behind the Wester Tower. You didn't even mention her husband's confession."

DeKok nodded.

"That's right," he said quietly. "You are right. I couldn't. I couldn't find the right opening. I just didn't know how."

Vledder wrinkled his nose slightly. "You ... you didn't know how?" he asked, unbelieving. "Act your age! Surely this isn't your first interrogation in a murder case?"

DeKok shrugged his shoulders.

"Really, I couldn't think of anything," he said, apologetically. He remained silent for a while; thinking, he plucked at his lower lip. "What should I have said? Mrs. Donkersloot did you know that last year your husband committed murder in Amsterdam ... did you know that your husband was a secret murderer ... how many nights has he been target shooting before he, and his pistol, went hunting?" It sounded rough and a bit cynical. "Or do you think I should have just shown her the confession?"

Vledder nodded emphatically.

"That is exactly what you should have done," he exclaimed, convinced. "You should have shown her the confession and asked her, at the same time, if that spidery handwriting was that of her husband." The young inspector became excited. "The only thing we've found out so far is that her husband, when in Amsterdam, sometimes stayed at the *Poort van Eden*. If you ask me, that's a sad result from a long trip to Rotterdam."

Resigned, DeKok let the critique from his younger colleague wash over him. It did not touch him. He, better than anyone, knew that his actions were not always rational. His brain did not happen to work like a pre-programmed computer. He was proud of that. By preference he liked to follow his instinct and his instinct told him that his approach to Mrs. Donkersloot had been right. He glanced aside and looked at the surly face of Vledder. Thoughtfully he rubbed his chin. How, so he thought, does one explain instinct. Softly groaning, he raised himself slightly in his seat.

"I don't think," he started carefully, "that Mrs. Donkersloot was aware of the criminal activities of her husband. He never told her anything. And learning from experience ... she never asked about his actions and business ... although she was, of course, very curious." The old detective spread his hands. "In addition, we don't really know if Sir Donkersloot's activities were indeed criminal."

Vledder grinned without joy: "The man committed murder ... criminal enough for you?"

DeKok sighed.

"What do we have to go on ..." he recapitulated patiently, " ... a menu from the *Poort van Eden* with the confession of a murder, found in an old history book of a deceased man. That's all. Do you know what the Law says? Prosecution expires with the death of the suspect. Well, the suspect is dead ... dead and buried. There is no longer a case. 'Dead on Arrival' they call that in the States." He was silent for a moment, took a deep breath. "But I don't believe it." His voice sounded irritated.

Vledder glanced at him: "What don't you believe?"

DeKok pressed his lips together.

"That the case should be dead and buried," he answered finally. "And I also don't believe that someone, without reason, ... as a kind of a hobby ... should write a confession about a murder he committed and that the

27

confession, as a sort of sick joke, should be stuck in an old history book. In my opinion, Donkersloot wasn't that type of person. He was a man with a philosophical bent ... a thinker. There had to be a reason for his actions."

Unconcerned, Vledder shrugged his shoulders.

"Read his confession. He felt the end was near and didn't want an innocent to pay for his crime."

DeKok reacted unusually emotional.

"Nonsense ... didn't feel the end was near. That is a complete lie. There was no question of a nearing end. According to his wife, Hendrik Peter Donkersloot was healthy as a horse ... never anything wrong."

Vledder frowned. "You think that the confession is a forgery?"

A painful expression appeared on DeKok's face.

"Hendrik Peter Donkersloot wrote in his confession that he fired three shots at Frederik van Ravenstein, with malicious intent and with full knowledge of the consequences, with an old Sauer 7.6mm. During the press conference at the time ... I didn't know then that the case was to be transferred to Narcotics ... I said, in order to protect myself against possible false confessions, that the body of Frederik Ravenstein had been found in the Prince's Canal with two bullet holes in his chest. That's what the newspapers reported."

Vledder looked at him with wide eyes. "There were three," he said.

DeKok nodded. "Exactly. And that is in agreement with the confession." He looked at his outstretched index finger. "And there is something else. During autopsy Dr. Rusteloos found a remaining bullet in the body of Frederik Ravenstein ... a 7.6mm."

Vledder's mouth fell open. "And those facts," he said surprised, "could only be known to the murderer."

Slowly DeKok nodded. "That's the way it is."

Vledder grinned: "So the perpetrator is Hendrik Peter Donkersloot, after all."

DeKok smiled: "I told you, the perpetrator is in the cemetery."

* * *

They drove past Schiphol Airport at a reasonable speed in their new Golf, passed the traffic snarls of Badhoevedorp and New Lake and entered old Amsterdam. The sun disappeared almost immediately and heavy raindrops descended from a dark, solid overcast sky. They exploded on the hood and rattled on the roof.

DeKok grinned: "That's how I know Amsterdam."

Vledder ignored the remark and started the wipers.

DeKok looked at the monotonous movement of the sweeping wipers and knew that in the new Golf they had the same hypnotic effect on him as, in the past, in the old Beetle. He closed his eyes and slid further down in the seat.

"You know how to find the station on your own?"

Vledder waved at the windshield.

"Blindfolded."

The old inspector chuckled.

"I'd keep my eyes open, if I were you," he said genially.

The young inspector decided on the same route in reverse. They passed the Nassau Square where the stone Domela Niewenhuis forever raises her arm in combat. The Haarlemmer Square had been taken over by gridlock and they progressed at a snail's pace. When they finally reached their destination, DeKok sighed with relief.

"Park that thing quickly. My dry throat can only be saved by cognac."

Almost automatically DeKok and Vledder strolled from the parking lot to the front of the station. In front of the bluestone stoop they halted, looked at each other for a few seconds and laughed. Then they moved sideways toward the Heintje Hoek Alley. Past *Onse Lieve Heer op Solder* (Our Dear Lord in the Attic), according to DeKok the dearest museum in the world, they walked straight to the Oude Zijds Voorburgwal.

It was quiet in the Red Light District. It was still too early for the lecherous and others were discouraged by the dense rain. Most of the brothels still had the curtains closed. On the Old Church Square a middle aged whore was knitting behind her window. She waved as the twosome passed by.

They crossed over the quaint old bridge of the Old Acquaintance Alley and on the corner of Barn Street they entered, almost furtively, the intimate bar of Little Lowee.

DeKok longed for a few shots from the bottle of Napoleon Cognac that Lowee kept special for him under the counter. Cognac stimulated his thinking and he felt that his brain needed the stimulation. The strange confession on the back of the menu irritated him. His instinct told him there was something wrong, but his reason told him there were no grounds to support his instinct.

Little Lowee wiped his hands on a soiled apron and approached them happily. "I am so glad to see you again," he chirped, "It's been a long time. Did the commissaris put you on the wagon?"

DeKok hoisted himself on a stool and shook his head.

"I don't let the commissaris tell me what to do," he answered moodily. "It's just been so damned busy, lately. It's almost impossible to regularly visit your ... eh, your reputable establishment." He stretched out his arm and poked Little Lowee playfully in the chest with an index finger. "Do your duty."

The barkeeper obeyed with the willingness of a good publican. In almost a single motion, he slid underneath the bar, grabbed three big snifters from behind him and poured.

Benignly beaming, DeKok looked at him. He loved these moments. Although he knew that the small barkeeper was a receiver of stolen goods, a thief and a man who had, during his lifetime, broken virtually all of God's Commandments ... he loved Little Lowee.

"Proost!" He picked up his glass, rocked it slightly in his hand and sniffed the stimulating aroma of the cognac. Carefully he took a sip. Softly the velvet liquid poured past his parched throat. He looked at the glass and with a tender gesture placed it on the bar.

"Lowee," he said seriously, "put all sins behind you and repent. I want to be able to meet you in Heaven."

The friendly, mousy face of Little Lowee grinned. "As barkeeper?"

DeKok nodded: "Exactly, that's what I mean."

The slender barkeeper sipped from his glass. "Working on a new murder?" he asked innocently.

DeKok shook his head. "Not a new one, an old one ... from last year. The murder of Frederik Ravenstein."

Little Lowee frowned. "Isn't your Narcotics Division working on that?"

DeKok looked at him, surprised. "How do you know?"

"They were here, then ... last year, at the beginning of August. They wanted information."

"About what?"

"Frederik Ravenstein."

31

"Did you know him?"

Little Lowee shrugged. "Whadda you mean by 'know'? Personally I never met him. But in my establishment you hear things. According to rumors he was one of the big financiers in the drug business. With a few others he controlled all of it. They say he didn't touch it himself. He left that to lesser lights. He just made fortunes from the business ... fortunes from the misery of the addicts." Emotion colored the voice of the slender barkeeper. "It was a blessing for Mankind that he was cut down."

"Any idea who did it?"

Little Lowee shook his head.

"As for that, as far as I know, nothing has leaked." He looked at the old investigator. "Do you really want to know?"

"Yes."

The bar owner grimaced: "Just be careful. It's a dangerous environment."

DeKok smiled at his worried tone.

"What did you advise the Narcotics people at the time?"

Little Lowee made an expansive gesture.

"To start fishing where the big boys regularly meet."

"And where is that, pray tell?"

"The *Poort van Eden.*"

4

With the light glow of cognac warming their blood and the cockles of their hearts, the two detectives left the dimly lit establishment of Little Lowee. Business had picked up in the Red Light District. The rain had stopped and the regular evening parade, past the windows filled with beckoning ladies, was getting into full stride. In the flattering light of discreetly placed pink and red spotlights, the women appeared to be of an attractive and sensual beauty. They all looked desirable.

Every once in a while a veritable congregation would collect in front of a particular window, whenever one of the younger whores, in an enterprising attempt to obtain more than her fair share of the business, would display a little more of the female form than was normally expected.

DeKok smiled in memory. That wouldn't have happened in the old days. The old-time whores would never have allowed such unfair competition and the errant entrepeneuse would quickly have been called to order. But the old-fashioned whores had almost all disappeared. It was mostly young flesh, that was being advertised these days, also a lot of exotic imports.

They arrived back at the station after leisurely threading their way through the narrow streets of the well-known neighborhood.

The bent finger of Jan Kusters, the desk sergeant, motioned them to come closer as they entered. DeKok approached the desk and spread his hands in a question.

"What's the problem?"

The sergeant came from behind the desk.

"There's a young man waiting for you upstairs."

"For me?"

Kusters nodded emphatically.

"He specifically asked for Inspector DeKok."

The old sleuth pushed the sleeve of his raincoat aside and looked at his watch.

"That's impossible! According to the laws governing the normal work week, I am not even supposed to be here."

Jan Kusters laughed.

"Normal work week! Come off it, you've never paid attention to that before, either coming, or going."

DeKok ignored the remark.

"Why did you let him go upstairs?" he asked accusingly. "You couldn't have known I'd be back tonight."

The sergeant pointed upstairs.

"The young man was certain that you would return to your place of employment tonight. He was absolutely convinced that you would still be working."

DeKok rippled his eyebrows in a most interesting manner.

"He said that?" he asked astonished.

Kusters nodded.

"According to him you are in the middle of a most important case."

"Did he leave his name?"

The sergeant shook his head.

"To be absolutely honest, I didn't even ask him," he said apologetically. " 'Just wait upstairs on the bench', I said, 'but if he hasn't shown in about an hour, I'd go home if I were you, because he won't be back tonight.'."

DeKok turned away from the desk. With Vledder in his wake, he climbed the stone steps to the third floor with a remarkable agility.

On the bench, next to the door of the large detective room at the end of the long corridor, they found a young man. DeKok estimated him to be in his early thirties. He wore a green trench coat of the style made popular by so many movie detectives. As soon as the young man spotted the old inspector, he rose and met them half way.

"My name is Evert Waterman," he called cheerfully. Offering his hand, he continued: "You're Inspector De-Kok?"

DeKok nodded with old-world decorum

"That's with ... eh, Kay-Oh-Kay."

The young man smiled.

"They told me you would say that!"

DeKok appraised him silently. Evert Waterman, he concluded, had a friendly open face with a broad chin, sparkling, light blue eyes and blond, curly hair.

"Who are 'they'?"

"People with whom I have discussed you."

DeKok grinned.

"I wasn't aware," he quipped, "that I would ever be the subject of a discussion."

Waterman nodded.

"As soon as I learned that you were handling the Donkersloot case, I informed myself about you."

Again DeKok's eyebrows rippled in that peculiar manner.

"What case am I handling?"

Evert Waterman, suddenly confused, looked at the Inspector: "The ... eh ... the Donkersloot case."

DeKok cocked his head.

"Is there such a thing? I mean, is there a ... what was it again ... eh, a Donkersloot case?" he asked with barely concealed amazement in his voice.

The young man was visibly perturbed.

"Yes, I mean, you ... eh, weren't you in Rotterdam, this afternoon? You went to see ... my aunt, didn't you?"

Surprised, DeKok looked at him.

"Mrs. Donkersloot in Rotterdam is your aunt?"

"Indeed so. My aunt. She is the widow of Hendrik Peter Donkersloot, my uncle ... the oldest brother of my mother. I have been named after him, in a way, my middle name is Hendrik, like his."

DeKok led the young man into the detective room and seated him on the chair next to his desk. Then he took off his raincoat. With a swashbuckling gesture he threw his hat at the peg and missed by at least two feet. In fact, he always missed. With a groan and a sigh, he bent over, picked up the much abused headgear, placed it on the hat rack with an excess of ceremony and shuffled over to his desk. Meanwhile his brain worked overtime. The visit and the statements of Evert Hendrik Waterman had surprised him, to say the least.

He sank down into the chair behind the desk and smiled at the young man.

"And what," he began, "is the substance of the so-called Donkersloot case, according to you?" His tone was friendly. almost solicitous.

Young Waterman waved in his direction with an expansive gesture.

"The books ... the book collection of my uncle."

"What do you mean by that?"

Waterman looked startled.

"You don't know?"

DeKok slowly stroked his nose with the tip of his pinky. It seemed to absorb him.

"I don't know," he finally said, carefully, "if we're talking about the same thing."

This time Waterman frowned, but he couldn't hope to equal the same interesting effect that DeKok achieved without effort.

"But didn't you go to Rotterdam in connection with my uncle's book collection?"

There was suspicion in his voice.

DeKok looked at the young man searchingly.

"Who says so?"

Waterman made a vehement gesture.

"Aunt! She said that the trail of the theft led to Amsterdam. You, Inspector DeKok of the Amsterdam police, had taken over the case from the Rotterdam police and you would find out what happened to the book collection."

For a change, DeKok rubbed his chin this time.

"Your aunt," formulating his response carefully, he continued: "Your aunt, reported to the Rotterdam police that the book collection was stolen?"

Waterman nodded.

"It is, after all, *my* collection."

"Yours?"

Again Waterman nodded. Emphatically.

"It was meant to be mine. I was supposed to inherit the book collection, if my uncle died. He promised. It's in his will, somewhere."

"And now the collection has been stolen?"

Again Evert Waterman looked at him suspiciously.

"You know that!"

DeKok sidestepped the observation.

"When was it stolen?"

"On the day of the funeral. I think that the burglars saw the announcement in the paper and thus used the day of the funeral to remove the book collection. They knew they wouldn't be disturbed."

"Was the collection valuable?"

"It was to me."

"In what way?"

"As a memory of my uncle. Uncle Henry was a very dear man, who paid a lot of attention to me, ever since I was little. He and aunt never had any children of their own. Sometimes I felt that my uncle looked upon me as his own son. I was devastated when aunt told me that the collection had been stolen."

Thoughtfully DeKok stared at nothing in particular. In his mind's eye he saw again the old house in Rotterdam ... the tall, thin old woman, dressed in black with the tightly pulled-back, grey hair. Calmly she had sat across from him. In a comfortable chair on a dull, bare parquet floor.

He could not reconcile that image. There was no depth. There was a dimension missing ... as if it had been a dream. Slowly the images faded away into the background. Back to the dusty recesses of his memories.

He tilted his head and looked sideways at the young man on the chair next to his desk. Suddenly a wild thought crossed his mind. It hit him like a stroke of lightning. His sharp eyes focused on the young man's face. Tense he waited for a reaction ... each little tremor of the skin, each slight shift of the eyes.

"Evert Hendrik Waterman," he asked evenly, "Do you like history?"

* * *

Vledder looked at DeKok and grinned.

"I told you, you were off your stride this afternoon, in Rotterdam. That old aunt in Rotterdam took you for a ride."

The old detective looked at him.

"Did she indeed report the theft of the book collection?"

Vledder nodded.

"I just got off the phone. According to the Rotterdam police her story was extremely believable. It wasn't the first time that people, upon returning from a funeral, found the premises ransacked. It seems to be something peculiar to Rotterdam."

DeKok rubbed his chin.

"An extremely shrewd and intelligent woman, the widow Donkersloot. I am beginning to doubt the story of the rest home, she's supposed to enter."

Vledder came closer.

"You mean," he exclaimed, wondering, "It may be a lie? She's not planning to go to a rest home, at all?"

DeKok nodded agreement.

"I think it possible that the rest-home story is just that, another story."

"But why?"

"It would provide an acceptable motive to cash in on all sorts of chattel."

Vledder grinned.

"Including the extensive book collection of your late husband, complete with confession of murder most foul, committed by the same late husband."

DeKok nodded.

"For instance," he agreed. "It's also a patent method to disappear completely from a certain environment, without awkward questions being asked." He thought for a while and then asked: "Did you inform Rotterdam that the reported theft was a false alarm?"

Vledder shook his head.

"In connection with the confession we found, I didn't think that would be a very wise thing to do."

DeKok winked.

"Very good," he praised. "It's better if Rotterdam doesn't know for a while. I don't want her approached for a false report. That could hamper our own investigations." His face contorted itself, as if in pain. "Still, to tell you the truth, I don't understand it at all, at all. Why ... why a false report?"

Vledder shrugged his shoulders.

"Perhaps the collection was more valuable then we think. Perhaps it was highly insured."

"You seriously mean to tell me that Mrs. Donkersloot was trying to put one over on the insurance company?"

"Why not?"

DeKok looked thoughtful.

"We'll have to check it out, of course," he said slowly. "but that motive for filing a false report somehow doesn't sit right with me. Also, I don't believe that the collection was all that valuable. Neither the remarks made by Jan Schouten, nor what Waterman tells us about the collection, give any indication of that. It was certainly a voluminous collection and Waterman probably attaches some sentimental value to it. But that's all. I mean, there were no art books, or rare books involved."

Vledder reacted exasperated.

"But there has to a be a reason for the false theft report. Mrs Donkersloot must have had something in mind."

In order to help his concentration, DeKok closed both eyes halfway. He struggled to place himself in the position of the old lady ... to try and understand her situation. "The question remains," he said, slowly formulating his statement, "if Mrs. Donkersloot was aware that her nephew would inherit the collection, after the death of her husband."

Vledder nodded vaguely, wondering where this was leading.

"I think she knew. I have to assume that. Positively. It is more than probable that a married couple would discuss that sort of thing."

DeKok gestured in his direction.

"Then she also had to know that, at the moment of her husband's death, the collection was no longer hers. Yet she made a false report, when the ownership had already gone to her nephew."

"So, what does that mean?"

DeKok stared again thoughtfully at nothing at all.

"It means a lot, yes, a lot, I think."

Vledder slapped the top of his desk rhythmically with the flat of his hand.

"But what?" he demanded impatiently.

DeKok stretched his index finger in front of him and looked at it.

"Although she knew that the collection would go to Nephew Evert after her husband's death, she allowed book seller Schouten to remove the collection from her home. She told her nephew that the collection was stolen on the day of the funeral and ... in order to make him believe that, she filed a false report with the police." He stopped talking and sighed, then: "That means to me just one thing ... Mrs. Donkersloot is determined to prevent her husband's book collection from falling into the hands of her nephew."

Vledder looked at him, questioning.

"But why?"

DeKok grinned.

"And that, Dick Vledder, seems an extremely intelligent question to me."

5

Casually greeting the desk sergeant as they passed his desk, they walked into the street. DeKok looked up. A steady drizzle descended from an overcast sky with the appearance of grey flannel. The drops stuck to his face.

The old inspector growled a curse. Tired, and pre-occupied with the strange confession from an old history book, he had been unable to fall asleep until very late. Even then he had suddenly woken up from a nightmare wherein a murdering old lady, jeering and laughing, had been chasing him.

Again DeKok looked at the sky. The weather, he thought, was not going to improve his disposition. He pushed his hat slightly forward and put up the collar of his raincoat.

From the Warmoes Street they turned right, into the Old Bridge Alley, with death defying arrogance they crossed the busy Damrak and dragged themselves along the pavement amidst a crowd of plastic wrapped holiday makers and tourists.

Vledder looked at the facades of the buildings.

"Do you know where it is, the *Poort van Eden*?"

DeKok nodded.

"On the Emperor's Canal, not too far from the Heart Street. I've been there once before ... a long time ago. In connection with a suicide. Old man Boorstang was still the manager at the time. He was a man who liked the police."

Vledder grinned.

"In that case he must be dead."

DeKok ignored him.

"Now they've new management," he continued, as if Vledder had not said a thing, "According to the hotel police, the interior has been radically changed ... renewed ... modernized. The clientele, also, has undergone a remarkable metamorphosis. Before you found there mostly simple folks on a budget, small business men, travelling sales people. Now they only cater to managers, directors, captains of industry."

Vledder sniffed.

"And the guys who finance the drug trade on the sly."

DeKok nodded.

"According to our friend Little Lowee ... and he's usually well informed. At least that's been my experience. We should talk to him at length, one of these days, about the drug trade. Also, as soon as possible, I want to see the files from Narcotics."

"About Ravenstein's murder?"

"Exactly ... I want to know what they found out, what sources have been tapped. I don't want to re-invent the wheel and cover their tracks all over again."

They passed the Royal Palace and in due course arrived at the Emperor's Canal. After just a few steps, DeKok suddenly stopped in his track. He turned and with a wide wave of the arm he pointed at the Wester Tower. The beautiful contours of the old church could just be discerned in the haze that was settling on the roof tops.

"The place of the murder and the *Poort van Eden*, within a stone's throw of each other."

* * *

The manager led the two detectives to the office of the President and Managing Director of the *Poort van Eden*, who greeted them condescendingly. He waved in the direction of two chairs in front of his desk and looked, with a meaningful glance, at his watch.

"My name is Boning, Arnold Boning," he said in a rush. "As you probably have been informed by my manager, I am the Managing Director here. I do hope that the gentlemen will have the goodness to take just a minimum of my valuable time. The running of a concern like this, does take my full attention and time."

DeKok grinned.

"Time," he said absent mindedly, "is a strange concept. Only a few seconds are usually necessary to commit murder. But the solving of a murder, believe me, it can sometimes take our full attention and time."

There was mockery in his tone of voice.

Arnold Boning looked at him searchingly.

"And that's why you are here ... murder?"

DeKok nodded.

"The murder of Frederik Ravenstein."

The director reacted with astonishment.

"But some gentlemen of your service have already been here for that very purpose."

"From Narcotics?"

"Yes, and you ..."

"From the Warmoes Street, Homicide."

Boning looked annoyed.

"Those kind of subtle differences are of no interest to me," he answered testily. "I can only tell you what I told your colleagues from, eh, Narcotics, at the time. Our hotel, the *Poort van Eden* has absolutely nothing to do with the death of Mr. Ravenstein. There is simply no connection, whatsoever."

DeKok smiled.

"It didn't take you long to come to that conclusion." He leaned slightly forward. "Wasn't Mr. Ravenstein, at the time of his death," he gambled, "registered as a guest in your hotel?"

Arnold Boning became red in the face.

"But that's an unimportant detail," he protested hotly, "whether the man was a guest, or planned to be a guest, what does it matter?"

DeKok ignored the question.

"Are you familiar with Mr. Ravenstein's activities?"

"What do you mean?"

"I mean, what was his business ... anything about his acquaintances, his associates?"

Mr. Boning was getting upset. His corpulent body shook with barely controlled anger and his chair creaked.

"This is a hotel, not a boarding house for school boys," he yelled loudly. "I couldn't care less about what my guests do for a living, or who they do it with, that's none of my business. As far as I'm concerned they all robbed the Bank of England, or ... eh ... I mean ..." He was unable to complete the sentence.

DeKok smiled a bitter smile.

"...or traffic in drugs?"

Arnold Boning gave a deep sigh. His small, sunken eyes were full of hate. The bright red color slowly faded from his face. Anger gave way to cool observation.

"You pose the most impossible questions," he said calmly, shaking his head. "Questions that I cannot answer. I am not responsible for the behavior of my guests." Slowly he rose from his chair. "I repeat ... for the last time ... our hotel, the *Poort van Eden*, has nothing to do with the death of Mr. Ravenstein. I wish to be spared any further police visits concerning this matter."

DeKok remained seated. Demonstratively. Slowly and almost insultingly he looked at the man. The fat, red, fleshy face with low-slung chins repulsed and disgusted him. The old sleuth was also trying to suppress a feeling of irritation that the heavy director was trying to achieve with his condescending manner. With some difficulty, DeKok produced a smile.

"Mr. Boning," he asked with his most winning smile and in his friendliest tone, "did you know a Mr. Donkersloot?"

"Donkersloot?"

DeKok nodded.

"Hendrik Peter Donkersloot, an older gentleman. According to my information he used to stay frequently in your hotel."

* * *

It was still raining when they left the *Poort van Eden*, but DeKok's disposition had improved markedly.

Despite the reluctant, almost non-existent cooperation from the managing director, the old inspector was not dissatisfied. During the interview he had become convinced that fat Arnold Boning knew a lot more about the affair than he was ready to admit. A sardonic smile played around the lips of the grey sleuth. He was unable to guarantee Boning that he would be spared further visits from the police.

Vledder looked at him from the side.

"I thought it was rather stupid of Boning to tell us that he didn't know Donkersloot. Without even trying very hard, I saw the name "Donkersloot" several times in the Guest Register." He stopped talking, obviously in order to achieve some sort of effect. "And you want to know something else?"

"What?"

"He also stayed there the night that Ravenstein was killed."

DeKok did not react immediately.

"I'm sure that the guys from Narcotics went through the Register with a fine toothed comb, at the time. They didn't make the connection."

Vledder snickered.

"Yes, but *they* didn't have a confession on the back of a Menu. But we do! Anyway, the fact that Donkersloot stayed in the *Poort van Eden* puts him suspiciously close to the scene of the crime."

DeKok smiled.

"Within a stone's throw." He was fond of that type of expression. They seemed to amuse him.

Vledder nodded emphatically.

"Exactly! I don't know what you think, but I am starting to take that confession seriously. And if we can prove blackmail as the motive for the murder, the case is closed."

DeKok grinned.

"And the perpetrator is in the cemetery."

Vledder listened carefully to the ironic tone.

"Don't you believe that Donkersloot is well and truly dead?"

DeKok laughed out loud.

"Oh, yes, he's indeed dead and buried. I checked that, just to be on the safe side. No doubt about it. Ever since the case with the Holy Order of Dying, over in Antwerp, I've become extremely careful about such matters."*

Vledder looked at him searchingly.

"So, what's bothering you?"

DeKok gestured violently.

"The truth!"

"Don't you believe that Donkersloot wrote the confession?"

DeKok sighed.

"It isn't that," he answered annoyed, "I'm sure that Donkersloot composed and wrote the confession himself. We will have to get some other samples of his handwriting and have it checked by an expert, just to be sure, but that won't create any surprises."

"What will?"

"I just don't believe that Donkersloot did the actual killing."

Totally surprised, Vledder looked at him.

"But then why the confession?"

DeKok nodded slowly.

"Indeed ... why the confession? That question has been tormenting me ever since Jan Schouten showed me the menu for the first time. If we knew the answer to that question ... the case would probably be solved on the spot."

For a while they walked on in silence. Despite the steady rain, it was busy in the inner city. A babel of foreign languages buzzed all around them. Although the town carried a reputation for excessive crime, Amsterdam remained one of the "must-see" places for most tourists.

They retraced their steps and arrived back in the station. DeKok stopped in the lobby, took off his hat and waved it at Kusters, the desk sergeant. Much to his surprise, for once, Kusters had no urgent messages for him.

With Vledder in his wake, he climbed the stone stairs to the third floor. No sooner did they enter the large detective room, when the phone on DeKok's desk started to ring.

The old detective could not suppress a boyish grin.

"It's as if they knew we just came in."

Vledder passed him and picked up the receiver.

The young detective listened for just a few seconds. He replaced the receiver. His face was serious. DeKok looked at him.

"Who was that?"

"Evert Waterman."

"And?"

Vledder swallowed.

"Aunt Donkersloot has disappeared without a trace."

---

* See: DeKok and Murder on Blood Mountain.

6

DeKok rippled his eyebrows in that inimitable manner.

"Without a trace?"

Vledder nodded.

"According to Evert Waterman. He went to see his aunt this morning, wanting to talk about his uncle's book collection. He found the house on Mill Lane deserted and completely empty. And not a trace of old aunt Donkersloot."

DeKok divested himself of his wet raincoat, hung it on a peg and shuffled over to his desk.

"Call City Hall and the Post Office in Rotterdam, when you have a chance. Perhaps she left a forwarding address."

Vledder looked at him, quizzically.

"Do you really expect that?"

DeKok shook his head.

"It seems to me that aunt Donkersloot doesn't just want to keep old Henry's book collection from her nephew, but she doesn't want to see him any more, either." He though for a while and then continued: "I would have liked to interview her once more."

"Regarding the false report?"

DeKok nodded.

"That too. But also regarding her completely changed attitude toward nephew Evert. Ever since her old man died, the relationship seems to have cooled considerably. I wonder, what can the reason be!" He was silent again and sat down behind the desk. "And something else ... I had a nightmare last night ... I dreamt about a horrible old lady that was chasing me, jeering and laughing. The lady was tall and thin, wore a black dress and had silver grey hair, put up in a chignon."

Vledder nodded.

"Widow Donkersloot!"

"My nightmare!"

Vledder sniggered.

"Did she tell you why she was chasing you?"

DeKok laughed.

"No, more is the pity, before I could ask her, I woke up."

There was a knock on the door and Vledder called: "Enter!"

The door opened slowly and a hefty man entered. He wore a dripping, dark blue, plastic raincoat. He wiped the water from his face and balding head with a white handkerchief. Hesitatingly, he approached DeKok.

The grey sleuth at once recognized the manager of the *Poort van Eden*. With astonishment on his face he rose from his chair and pointed invitingly to the chair next to his desk.

"A complete surprise ... I must say. Did the director send you?"

Shaking his head, the man sat down, unbuttoned his dripping raincoat with shaking fingers and looked up at DeKok.

"I ... eh, I come on my own. I just took some time off. I ... eh, I want to talk to you." Obviously ill at ease, he looked at young Vledder and added: "Confidentially."

DeKok sat down and made a soothing gesture.

"This is my colleague, Vledder," he said in a friendly tone, "also my assistant and extremely trustworthy. I keep no secrets from him."

The man re-arranged himself on the chair.

"I, eh, that is, I greeted you, but I did not introduce myself. My name is Valenkamp ... Peter Valenkamp. But I'd rather you forget the name as soon as possible."

DeKok looked a question.

"And what do you mean by that?"

Valenkamp made an apologetic gesture.

"I already told you ... my message is of a confidential nature."

DeKok spread his hands.

"So confidential, that I couldn't use it in a public trial?"

Valenkamp nodded.

"Exactly. That's what I mean. I don't feel like being fished out of some canal with a few bullets in my body. And that's likely."

DeKok worried with the tip of his nose.

"Like, for instance, the late Mr. Ravenstein?"

Peter Valenkamp nodded again. Slowly and thoughtfully.

"Like," he repeated, "the late Mr. Ravenstein."

The hotel manager paused a moment and then changed his tone. "I've been at the *Poort van Eden* since Mr. Boorstang's time. He's the one who promoted me to manager." A tender smile, fled across his lips. "A fine man, old Mr. Boorstang. During his time the *Poort van Eden* was still a fine hotel. A hotel for nice people."

"And that isn't so any longer?"

Valenkamp shook his head.

"The gentlemen who currently frequent the hotel aren't my friends. I didn't come here to gossip ... please don't take it that way." He raised his arm and touched his neck with the side of his hand. "But I've had it up to here, with the current shenanigans ... I've been wanting to talk about it for some time, now ... I just couldn't take the final step. But when I saw you again, this morning ..." He did not complete the sentence. "Arnold Boning is no good," he continued, "he isn't worth a plugged nickel. Right after you left he went crazy on the telephone. One call after an another. For more than an hour. I came in to discuss tomorrow's menu with him and he practically chased me out of his office."

"You don't know who he was talking to? What city?"

"I don't know, he's got a direct line. His calls are not recorded by the switch board."

DeKok assessed him silently.

"And ...eh, your dissatisfaction," he asked carefully, "is mainly with the new ownership, the new direction the hotel has taken?"

Valenkamp shook his head.

"It's the whole rotten clique ... people who make fortunes in drugs ... who thrive on the misery of others. That's the money that took over the *Poort van Eden* ... that's what financed the remodelling. The hotel has become the unofficial headquarters of the European drug traffic."

DeKok cocked his head.

"And ... Arnold Boning belongs to that group? He's part of it?"

Valenkamp nodded emphatically.

"After Ravenstein's murder, last year, he's become the king pin."

DeKok's eyebrows rippled dangerously.

"Ravenstein was the original boss of the group?"

Peter Valenkamp pressed his lips together and then said, almost whispered:

"Yes, indeed. And I wouldn't be at all surprised if Boning planned the murder of Ravenstein."

"But hired someone else to do it?"

Valenkamp grinned sardonically.

"What do you expect ... that fat bastard wouldn't dirty his own hands with a killing."

DeKok gestured in his direction.

"Where there controversies, conflicts ... tension?"

The other looked serious.

"There were some rumors as long ago as early last year, about a planned settling of accounts. Perhaps a dissolution of the partnership. They still met regularly at the hotel, but for some time now, I don't think they got along at all well, the four of them." In response to DeKok's look, he added: "Boning, Teest, Ravenstein and Donkersloot."

With a sudden movement DeKok leaned forward over his desk.

"You said Donkersloot?"

Valenkamp nodded.

"Yes, Donkersloot, yes, he was one of them, too."

* * *

It took several seconds for DeKok to absorb the full import of the message. Here, at least, was a reasonable explanation for Donkersloot's many visits to the *Poort van Eden* in Amsterdam. Yet, the thought that Donkersloot was a prominent member of a crime syndicate, shocked him. He had never had that impression, not even a suspicion ... not even after Little Lowee told him about the connection between drugs and the *Poort van Eden*.

"Is Donkersloot dead?" he asked absent mindedly and totally superfluous.

Valenkamp nodded.

"A sudden heart attack, I heard." The manager looked guilty. "Perhaps it sounds strange, but I was a bit sorry to hear about his sudden death. Among that filthy bunch, Donkersloot was different ... always friendly ... interested ... always a nice word for everybody. I never really understood why such a man would associate himself with that filthy business." Suddenly he smiled. "Would you believe it? At one time I was actually about to ask him that very question?"

"You were intrigued?"

"Exactly! That's the right word. It just didn't seem to suit the man."

DeKok leaned forward gain.

"Have you any idea about the cause of the controversies, the conflicts, in the group?"

Valenkamp shrugged his shouldered.

"The conferences among the gentlemen were, after all, very secret. I wasn't allowed to participate. But if the gentlemen needed service, food, drinks, whatever, then I was the only one allowed to do so. Usually they stopped talking as soon as I entered, but sometimes I caught a stray word, here and there."

"Such as?"

"That Donkersloot wanted to retire from the group."

"And the others didn't agree?"

A painful look came over the hotel manager.

"I don't know," he answered, "I was never too clear about that. But there was a lot of tension in the group. Especially Ravenstein and Teest used to argue a lot ... Donkersloot used to act as peacemaker. It is as if they didn't trust each other ... as if they were cheating each other.

Therefore I wasn't too surprised by the murder of Ravenstein."

DeKok nodded agreement.

"I understand. You expected some sort of explosion?"

Somberly, Valenkamp agreed.

"It had to happen. Boning must have composed one of his infamous menus."

At a loss as to the meaning of this cryptic remark, DeKok looked at him, barely controlling his eyebrows.

"Menus?"

Peter Valenkamp nodded.

"Normally the chef puts the menus together ... usually in consultation with myself and Boning, of course. But sometimes, Arnold Boning creates a menu all by himself. Extensive menus are then being put together ... complicated menus with many courses."

DeKok looked confused. He shook his head and the eyebrows were now definitely rippling as he looked at the manager.

"I ... eh," he spoke hesitatingly, "I ... eh, to be honest, I don't know what you're talking about. I don't understand what you mean."

Valenkamp smiled, almost condescendingly, but his expression changed quickly.

"I'm not exactly sure how it works, myself," he hesitated, "I've, of course, never been told. I also don't know the code. But I do know that none of the group ever, actually, had any contact with the suppliers ... the couriers ... with the people that ran the real risks. I find it easy to believe that the ladies and gentlemen probably don't even know each other. But, as far as I have been able to figure out, the orders, messages and contracts are being passed along via the special menus in the restaurant."

DeKok gaped speechless at the hotel manager. When he found his voice, he said:

"Via the menu? For everyone to see?"

Valenkamp nodded agreement.

"If you know the code ... you'll know the messages buried in the special, complicated menus."

DeKok took a deep breath.

"And anybody who knows the code," he formulated his thoughts slowly, as if wanting to make sure to get it right, "can just read the menu and get his, or her, instructions, will know the wishes of the bosses, the money men, and act accordingly."

"That's right."

DeKok thoughtfully stroked his wide chin. Then he pointed at the hotel manager.

"And you're reasonably sure," he asked, "that Boning gave his instructions for the untimely demise of Ravenstein via one of these coded menus?"

Valenkamp's face became expressionless.

"That's what I think, yes."

Astounded, DeKok closed his eyes.

"Murder," he said softly. His voice trembled a little. "Murder on the menu."

7

A deep silence fell over the large detective room after Peter Valenkamp left. DeKok had advised the hotel manager to remain at the *Poort van Eden*, to continue his regular duties and to be, above all, very careful not to betray his suspicions against his employers, neither by word, nor by deed. The grey sleuth did not think it all unlikely that Boning would be capable of drastic revenge, if pressed. In the world of drug trafficking one life, more or less, was hardly noticed. Death sentences were pronounced without any further thought and just as casually executed. It was called liquidation, or "containing the damage".

DeKok placed both elbows on the desk and rested his head in his hands. He was not pleased with the sudden developments and he contemplated passing his information on to Narcotics and then quietly withdrawing from the case.

But something stopped him ... a strange, uncomfortable feeling ... a vague realization, that the final solution was not to be found in Amsterdam, or in the *Poort van Eden*, but in a deserted brownstone on a up-scale street in Rotterdam.

Vledder finally broke the silence.

"You didn't show Donkersloot's confession to Valenkamp."

DeKok shook his head.

"I didn't think it wise," he explained. "I think it's better if the hotel manager keeps thinking that it was Boning who gave the orders for Ravenstein's killing. That will keep him alert. That's why I only showed him the front of the menu. I wanted to know if it was one of the special Boning menus, with a code imbedded."

"It was not."

DeKok sighed.

"Too bad, according to Valenkamp, Boning makes sure that the special menus are immediately destroyed the next day. I hope that he will be able to make good on his promise and that he will be able to keep one of them behind, in the near future. Boning cannot stop giving instructions, after all."

Vledder wrinkled his forehead.

"And what use is such a special menu to us?"

"I admit, it's a little vague. Valenkamp isn't even sure that messages are passed via the menus. But it seems likely. Perhaps he's right. But we just don't have any proof."

Vledder pulled up a chair and straddled it backwards. A look of petulance showed on his young face.

"I don't believe it," he said, shaking his head. "and it doesn't compute. If you consider the relationships in the so-called partnership, it's just not possible that Boning would instruct Donkersloot to kill Ravenstein by passing a message on a menu. Ravenstein was the leader and he would be familiar with the code. Also, there was no need to pass the message on in such a complicated way. They were regularly in contact with each other."

DeKok looked at him with genuine admiration.

"Very good," he commended, "very good. That's the first time, so far in this case, that you've come up with some really intelligent remarks. You're right, it does not compute. There's something seriously wrong with the whole set-up." He raised a warning finger. "But we have to be extremely careful. We should probably take Valenkamp's remarks with a grain of salt. At the same time, we cannot dismiss them. He obviously has an aversion, if that's the word, against the current ownership of the hotel. Mind you, I understand the aversion. I don't like Boning either. But that kind of dislike can easily lead to all sorts of imagined slights, or suspicions."

Vledder stuck his chin further into the room.

"Yet, I'm convinced that there are some strange things happening in and around the *Poort van Eden*."

DeKok nodded his head in agreement.

"We can safely assume that." He was silent, a thoughtful expression on his face. Then: "What do we know about the fourth man of the syndicate?"

"You mean Teest?"

"Exactly."

Vledder shrugged his shoulders.

"Not much ... not much more than the information from the hotel register at the *Poort van Eden*. Bert Teest, 33 years of age, lives in Edam. According to Valenkamp, the least noticeable of the illustrious four."

DeKok grinned maliciously.

"Of which only two are still alive!"

He paused. His brain worked overtime while he let the various facts and possibilities of the case, as far as known, pass in review.

"Give Narcotics a call, perhaps the name Teest rings a bell over there. Also check on Boning. They met him, after all. They should at least be aware of the activities at the *Poort van Eden*, even if they can't prove anything. I wonder, by the way, when they're planning to send us the files on Ravenstein."

Vledder snorted.

"They apparently didn't even question the manager, Valenkamp, that is, at the time. At the very least that was a mistake, perhaps even negligence. He might have been as forthcoming with them as he's been with us and they might just have solved the case."

There was a soft knock on the door of the detective room and the young inspector called: "Enter!" It sounded hard and irritated.

The door opened slowly. The figure of a young woman appeared in the door opening. She waited to emphasize the effect she made, hand on her hip, left hip slightly thrust forward. Then she strode toward the two men, slowly, with elegant movements.

DeKok stopped breathing, She was beautiful, he thought, exceptionally beautiful, almost a classical beauty, with a wealth of joyous curves, calculatingly displayed.

During her sensuous approach she removed a scarf from her head with a routine gesture. Long, gold blonde hair fell in shiny, luxurious waves around the shoulders of her shiny, fire-engine red raincoat.

Vledder rose and hastily pulled his chair forward. With old-world charm and a reserved bow, DeKok indicated the empty chair next to his desk. She thanked him with a sweet smile.

"You're Inspector DeKok?"

The grey sleuth nodded with a naughty twinkle in his eyes.

"With Kay-Oh-Kay," he answered without thinking.

Two well-manicured hands stroked her beautifully shaped posterior as she smoothed her dress and sat down.

She removed a stray strand of her glorious hair from in front of her face and with a sweet and searching look she stared at the old Inspector.

"You are generally known as an excellent detective," she started in a lilting voice. "That's why I am so glad that you have taken charge of the case. It's been more than a year. Perhaps there will finally be a solution."

DeKok's eyebrows started their rippling dance.

"What case?" he asked, startled. "Of what case I am supposed to have taken charge?"

A look of disappointment was not able to mar her beauty.

"Fatman," she explained apologetically. "he called me this afternoon ... he was really excited and he said that you are now taking care of Friedreich's case."

DeKok wrinkled his nose.

"Who is 'Fatman'?"

She laughed gaily.

"That's what we call him. Boning, Arnold Boning. He is, to say the least, rather well fleshed out, corpulent, overweight. Let's face it ... he's fat. So therefore: 'Fatman'!"

The grey sleuth nodded understanding. He looked at her again, with the eyes of a detective, this time, not those of a man. She was, he observed objectively, attractive, sensuous. But the bewitching influence that was so strong when she first had entered the room, was slowly fading ... it was being replaced by a businesslike, sober assessment.

"And who is your 'Friedreich'?"

A tender smile played fleetingly across her face.

"Frederik Ravenstein. That's his real name. But I always called him Friedreich *von* Ravenstein. He was of German origin, you know ... a real Prussian. He had such a nice, bald, gleaming head and he always walked with such a stiff neck." Grinning she pulled her head down into her collar. "it was as if he was always walking with a pair of binoculars in front of his face. You know what I mean?"

DeKok ignored the question. He was good at ignoring things, when he set his mind to it.

"And who are you?"

She laughed cheerfully.

"Anna, ... Anna Breitenbach, also of German origin. I still have family in Berlin. Perhaps that's why I got along so well with my stiff Friedreich."

DeKok leaned toward her.

"You were married to Frederik Ravenstein?"

Laughing, she shook her head.

"Mar-ried?" She made it sound like a dirty word. "I was his girl-friend, for years really." She looked up at him. "He had a wife and children, somewhere, but I've never seen or heard anything of them. Of course, I asked him about it, sometimes, but he never wanted to talk about it. He considered that period of his life a closed book. He had lost all contact ... with his wife and ... his children." Slowly, as if in thought, she nodded, thinking. "But he did support them. Every month a fat check ... more than enough, I thought."

DeKok did not like her contemptuous tone at all. His puritan soul rebelled. According to him, marriage was a holy institution, which might be mocked, of course, but always had to be respected.

"You lived together?"

Anna nodded with a certain emphasis.

"Almost seven years. I was happy with him ... I could do what I wanted."

"For example?"

"Clothes ... nice car. Going out a lot. Very chic, always. Wonderful, long vacations."

"Did you know how Frederik earned his money?"

Anna nodded again.

"Oh, yes, he was in business, with Fatman ... and others."

"What kind of business?"

Anna shrugged her beautiful shoulders. The light did interesting things to her hair as it moved.

"I don't know, exactly," she laughed, "The details never interested me. I never really asked him anything about his business. But then, he probably didn't expect me to."

"That you would ask questions?"

"Exactly! I was his pleasure and I did what he wanted, from time to time. It doesn't pay to want to know too much. What the eye doesn't see, the heart doesn't suffer, that's what my mother always used to say. He had money and in my own way I loved the rigid old duffer. He was almost like a father to me ... the father I never had ... never knew."

DeKok heard the tremor in her voice.

"Where do you live?"

Anna gestured vaguely around.

"Dear Friedreich had a nice little cottage near the beach. Happily for me, he took timely steps to take care of it, so that I could move right in, after he died." she sighed deeply. "He always used to *care* for me so much."

DeKok appraised her sincerity, as well as her figure.

"Did Frederik expect to die, or something? Is that why he took steps to provide for you?"

Anna's face became serious.

"We were afraid ... both of us."

DeKok closed his eyes half way.

"Why? Of whom?"

65

Anna rubbed the back of her neck. It was a gesture of extreme weariness. She closed her eyes and the long, golden hair fell like a curtain in front of her face.

"I already told them," she said softly, "I told the other police men all about it."

"You mean the officers from Narcotics?"

Slowly she nodded.

"But they never followed up on it. They probably didn't even investigate it."

"What?"

Anna Breitenbach released a deep sigh.

"I know who killed my Friedreich."

Vledder straightened himself. DeKok was all quivering attention.

"You know who killed Frederik Ravenstein?" His voice shook slightly with a mixture of hope and disbelief.

Without looking at either of the detectives, Anna sighed again and then said, tonelessly:

"Bert Teest ... he was ... he is still in love with me."

8

DeKok burst out laughing. It was a relief. "If every love affair would lead to murder, there wouldn't be enough room for jails in all of Holland!"

Anna did not laugh. Her face remained serious and somber. She looked at the old inspector with a stern, reproachful look in her eyes.

"You just don't know Bert Teest," she said, as if carrying the worries of the world on her shoulders. Her gay personality had completely disappeared. "You've never met him. But I can assure you ... he's a brute ... a man who will stop at nothing. My Friedreich was deadly afraid of him. He told me that he knew from experience, how pitiless Teest could be. According to Friedreich, Bert Teest, no matter that he's still young, has a long history of violence. If something ever happens to me, Friedreich used to say, I won't be his first victim."

DeKok was, despite himself, surprised by Anna's seriousness.

"Did Teest ever threaten Frederik directly?"

Anna shook her head.

"Not directly, but through me."

"How?"

67

Anna sighed deeply. It did interesting things to her figure, but neither of the men paid any attention.

"Let me try to tell you in chronological order ... otherwise it will just sound like crazy talk." She adjusted in her seat. "One day, about a year and a half ago, Friedreich and I went to Amsterdam. He had to attend some sort of meeting at the *Poort van Eden*. I was to spent my time shopping until he was through. When I went to meet him at the hotel, after an hour or so, Teest was there and Friedreich introduced us. Bert tried to put the make on me, almost from the start ... uncouth, openly ... in Friedreich's presence! I didn't have a quiet moment after that. He was always calling me on the phone and he would sent flowers almost every day."

DeKok's eyebrows vibrated like the antennae of an insect.

"What did Frederik do about it?"

"Poor Friedreich. He didn't like it, but he simply lacked the courage to confront Teest about it. He was afraid of him. Don't ever cross that Teest, he used to say, or you're bound to disappear."

"That bad?"

"Yes."

DeKok tilted his head and looked at her.

"So what did Frederik want you to do?" he asked unbelieving, "Did he want you to respond to Teest's advances?"

Offended, Anna shook her head.

"Absolutely not!" She was genuinely distressed at the thought. "Friedreich didn't want to lose me! Not for all the money in the world. But he did advise me to be extremely careful."

"And you were ... careful?"

"Yes."

"Did you encourage him at all?"

Anna reacted furiously.

"Encourage him!" she exclaimed contemptuously. "I loathed him! I don't like pushy young men. I'm not impressed with all that macho stuff. And I told him so. I made sure he understood that I would never leave my Friedreich ... even if he was a lot older than me." She raked her hair with spread fingers, it did nothing to mar the glory of the blonde cascades. "One day," she continued in a more subdued tone, "I met Teest in the city. Pure coincidence. I had been shopping and I was just coming out of a department store. He took me by the arm and practically forced me to join him on a terrace for some coffee. Because I didn't want to make a scene in the middle of the street, I went with him. He plied me what all sorts of proposals and wanted to know what I could possibly see in poor Friedreich. According to him, Friedreich was an old, used-up man, without any glamour. When I told him, for the thousandth time, or more, that I would not leave Friedreich, no matter what, he became very angry. 'Then there is only one thing left to do,' he said, 'if you don't want to leave him, I've to take steps for him to leave you, permanently.'." She clapped her hands in front of her face. "The next day Friedreich disappeared. He never came back home and a few days later his body was found in the Prince's Canal."

DeKok let her be. When she finally removed her hands from in front of her face, he could see tears in her eyes. He leaned toward her.

"Does Teest still bother you?"

She shuddered, sniffled and nodded her head.

"He still sends flowers and until a few weeks ago, he used to call daily. Since then I've changed my phone number to an unlisted number. At least his phone calls have stopped. And he doesn't dare approach me in person."

DeKok looked at her, surprised.

"And why not?" he asked.

"I told him, if he ever came near me, I'd shoot him down like a dog ... no matter where ... in the middle of the city, if needed."

"You have a weapon?"

Anna pressed her lips together. She thrust out her chin.

"A very good FN, 9mm," she remained silent for a while and then added: "And I know how to use it."

It sounded threatening.

"You are a member of a shooting club?"

She shook her head.

"Friedreich taught me how to shoot. He was crazy about weapons. We used to practice in the woods, behind the cottage. In winter we used to go to the beach for practice."

Savoring the memory, she allowed her lips to form into a tender smile. "Friedreich always thought that the Belgian FN, although it was a 9mm, was very much inferior to his favorite, an old German Sauer 7.6mm. He used to say that the Sauer is the best pistol ever made."

DeKok stroked his broad chin.

"Did you ever accuse Teest directly, I mean, did you ever tell him that you suspected him of Ravenstein's murder?"

Anna sat up straight and nodded affirmatively.

"A number of times ... almost every time he called. I also told him that I would tell the Narcotics people about my suspicions."

"And ... what did he say to that?"

"Just let them try to prove it. I'm not in the habit of doing sloppy work, or something like that."

DeKok gestured in her direction.

"Teest never denied that he was responsible for Ravenstein's death, did he?"

Again she shook her head.

"He never denied it, but he also never admitted it. But he did, on numerous occasions, hint that the Friedreich's death was a direct result of the love that he, Teest, had for me. And, of course, the fact that I had rejected his love." She closed her eyes and a powerful emotion made her lower lip tremble. "In fact, 'You are responsible for his death,' he used to say."

* * *

DeKok fell back into his chair. Anna Breitenbach had left, but the scent of her perfume still filled the air. Above his head a defect ballast hummed annoyingly in one of the light fixtures. A drunk, outside, attempted to sing a melancholy melody. It was, he reflected, apparently the fate of erotic women to either get into trouble, or cause trouble. Beauty was by no means always a blessing and most definitely not a guarantee for happiness.

The grey sleuth looked at Vledder, who was busily making notes and gave an appearance of great industry.

"When are we going to arrest Teest," he said tauntingly.

The younger man looked up.

"You believe her?"

DeKok nodded.

"I believe her."

Vledder acted surprised.

"You really believe that Teest killed Ravenstein?"

DeKok made him the recipient of one of his mild smiles.

"I believe that Anna Breitenbach believes that Teest killed Ravenstein and she now hopes that we can prove it. But it is remarkable that Ravenstein died almost immediately after Teest threatened Anna with that."

Vledder looked at him searchingly. Not for the first time, wishing he could read the other's mind.

"But you will keep the possibility in mind that Teest may really have killed Ravenstein?"

DeKok grinned. His face was very attractive when he did that.

"I keep every possibility in mind, for the time being," but he could not prevent a bit of uneasiness in his tone of voice. "Narcotics judged the murder of Ravenstein to be just one more liquidation in the drug world. Valenkamp points to Boning as the killer, in connection with a power struggle. Dear Anna accuses Teest because of a frustrated love affair, and dead old Donkersloot is so kind as to take the blame himself and mentions blackmail. It's like Wheel of Fortune! Keep spinning and something will come up, every time. Too many suspects and not enough bodies. If you see a solution, don't keep it to yourself."

Vledder shoved his notes aside.

"I don't see a connection," he said, shaking his head. "Frankly, the motive that Valenkamp came up with, seems the most plausible."

DeKok attacked his lower lip this time. Thoughtfully he pulled it out and let it plop back. A very annoying sound.

"A power struggle within the syndicate with Boning as the brains?"

Vledder nodded.

"Well, in a way, you could also classify that as a liquidation, according to Narcotics. But I just don't know how that can be reconciled with Donkersloot's confession. It just doesn't fit."

The young inspector rose from his chair with a wild, irritated movement.

"I've got the terrible feeling that we'll never find the solution," he cried exasperated. "It's impossible. We're a year behind the facts and we'll retire on this case, mark my words, And that ..."

He stopped his ranting.

The phone on DeKok's desk rang insistently. Vledder leaned forward and picked it up. He listened. The face of the younger man became a study in disappointment.

"Where?" he asked evenly.

Almost immediately thereafter he replaced the receiver.

DeKok looked up at him.

"Who was that?"

"Downstairs, desk sergeant."

"And?"

"They found a man behind the Central Station, at the end of Pier 27."

"Dead, of course?"

Vledder nodded.

"Murdered," he said.

* * *

A very young constable guarded the entrance to the pier. As soon as he spotted the two detectives, he walked toward them.

"The Thundering Herd has been alerted," he called cheerfully.

DeKok smiled at him. Everybody knew that 'Thundering Herd' was his name for the group of forensic experts, medical examiners, photographers and other specialists that were always called in when a dead body was discovered. This young constable could not have been on the force more than few months, yet already he had picked up some of the DeKok's peculiarities. DeKok had never seem him before. It was uncanny, he reflected, he knew he was old, but his colleagues made him feel ancient, sometimes.

"Excellent," was DeKok's only comment.

The young constable pointed at the patrol car, parked at some distance. "The man who discovered the body is in there. I thought I'd better keep him for you. He told me that he was taking a piss from the end of the pier, you can't see it from here, when he suddenly discovered a corpse next to him. He went in to the Railroad Station and reported it to one of the Railroad Police. They alerted us."

"You have his name?"

The young constable nodded.

"Here it is," he handed him a scrap of paper. "It will also be in our report," he concluded importantly.

DeKok looked around.

"Where's your partner?"

The constable pointed into the distance.

"At the end of the pier, with the body." He shook his head and grinned. "He must be afraid the corpse will try to run away."

DeKok ignored the remark. He didn't like the joke. Without another word, he passed the constable and entered the pier. It stank of tar and used oil. An old, rusty barge was tied up on the left. The weathered hemp ropes that moored

74

it, creaked. The dirty water of the harbor splashed against the bow, removing the last few slivers of paint. Past an old guard shack with boarded up windows, he reached the end of the pier and found a constable, only slightly older than his partner. The constable recognized him, touched his cap and pointed silently to the corpse at his feet. DeKok squatted down and looked at the dead man and was shocked. Even in the dimming twilight he immediately recognized the man.

Vledder leaned over him to get a closer look. He could feel the breath of the young Inspector in the back of his neck.

"That's ... eh, that's ..."

He was stumped.

DeKok opened the coat of the corpse and looked at the wounds. Slowly he rose to a standing position and nodded at Vledder.

"Arnold Boning," he said evenly, "with three bullets in the chest."

9

DeKok studied the corpse. Arnold Boning was supine. His large, round stomach stuck up into the air and his legs were slightly spread. The left arm, palm up, pointed at the water. The other arm was stretched alongside the magnitude of his body.

DeKok gestured around him.

"As soon as they have moved the corpse, we'll have to take a close look around for traces of dragging."

Surprised, Vledder looked at him.

"You expect to find that? You think they dragged him here?"

DeKok nodded thoughtfully.

"I suspect," he said reluctantly, "that the murderer wanted to drop the corpse into the water. It disappears for a few days and will delay discovery. It buys the perpetrator a considerable amount of time."

Vledder looked for confirmation.

"You mean, as with Ravenstein?"

"Exactly. They tried, but I think that Boning was a little too heavy. It's rather a mass of flesh."

"That means a single suspect?"

DeKok grinned.

"I've an idea that Boning was too much of a load, even for two men."

The grey sleuth looked out over the harbor. It was uncommonly busy on the wide, almost ripplefree water. Vacation, the first balmy summer evening of the season had taken hold. A stately, white cruise ship, brightly lit, was surrounded by a veritable armada of expensive yachts, pleasure boats, motor cruisers and crowded excursion boats.

Vledder pointed at the water.

"Could the killer have come by water?"

DeKok shrugged his shoulders.

"Possible ... some sort of floating contraption. But not necessarily. It seems more likely that Boning had an appointment here for a secret meeting with his killer, whoever he, or she, may be. This is just the spot for that sort of meeting."

Old Doctor Koning shuffled closer, closely followed by two morgue attendants, pushing the inseparable gurney. DeKok greeted Doctor Koning with a glad smile and outstretched hand. They had known each other for years and DeKok was extremely fond of the small, always eccentrically dressed, coroner. With his old-fashioned grey spats and striped pants, the decorous morning coat and the greenish Garibaldi hat, the coroner looked like the lone survivor of a previous century.

"How are you?" asked DeKok.

Doctor Koning growled.

"I don't know what's come over people, lately," he exclaimed pathetically. "This is my fifth corpse tonight ... the fifth. Sometimes I think that half the population is engaged in systematically wiping out the other half."

DeKok nodded agreement.

"It's because of the unholy drugs," he agreed somberly. "Amsterdam sometimes reminds me of Chicago during Prohibition. Murder with assembly line techniques."

Doctor Koning was getting excited.

"The American Prohibition was the biggest blunder in history! It took much, much too long, before they realized it. Twelve years! By that time thousands had been murdered and additional thousands died of methyl-alcohol poisoning."

DeKok placed a soothing hand on the shoulder of the old medical man.

"What about our current drug management?"

Doctor Koning did not answer. He pointed at the corpse on the pier.

"That's quite a mass of flesh," he grimaced.

He took his Garibaldi hat off, pulled up the pant legs of his striped trousers and knelt next to the corpse.

DeKok watched tensely.

The small coroner opened the flaps of the coat, unbuttoned the white silk shirt and looked at the bullet wounds. Three bullet holes. Close together ... within a circle of less than 3 inches.

Knees creaking, the old man rose. With finicky gestures he removed his old-fashioned glasses, took a silk handkerchief from his breast pocket and polished the glass.

"He's dead," he said laconically.

DeKok nodded agreement with an expressionless face.

"I was afraid of that."

Doctor Koning gestured in the direction of the corpse.

"But he hasn't been dead long. Body temperature is still relatively high. Hardly any drop in temperature." He looked up. "Did you see the bullet wounds?"

"Yes, three, bunched together."

"A good shot. I think that at least two of the bullets went through the heart." The coroner replaced his handkerchief, his glasses and his extravagant hat, turned around, waved a vague greeting and shuffled away.

DeKok stared after him and spotted Bram Weelen. The photographer walked toward him with a long stride. His aluminum suitcase, filled with the tools of his trade, was tucked under his right arm.

"You have any special wishes?" he asked hastily.

DeKok grinned. It was his most attractive feature.

"I know, I know, you've got to go somewhere, right?"

Weelen nodded. "A little get-together of the Bridge Club. Once a year we spent all the dues money. Really nice shindig. Wouldn't want to miss it."

"I think you just live from one party to the next, don't you?"

Weelen choose a camera from his collection with the eye of the connoisseur. He mounted a flash attachment.

"Ach, you have to know how to enjoy life." He flashed into the dead face of Arnold Boning. "There's not all that much time. Life is short, you know." He glanced briefly at DeKok, then added: "And perhaps I've seen too many dead faces."

DeKok ignored the remark. He watched carefully the shots taken by Weelen. When the photographer finished, he nodded his approval. Bram Weelen packed his stuff together, closed his aluminum companion and ran off the pier.

Ben Kruger looked after the hastily disappearing photographer, turned to DeKok and pointed his thumb over a shoulder.

"He was in a hurry, again, wasn't he?"

DeKok grinned agreement.

"A party."

The fingerprint man looked at the corpse, looked at the surroundings and pulled a face.

"Not much for me to do, here." He pointed at the dead man. "Do you have an identity yet?"

DeKok nodded: "Arnold Boning," he said.

"Have we got his fingers, you think?"

DeKok made a movement with his shoulders. "I don't think so. But take them, just to be sure. No rush. You can do it in the morgue, tomorrow, before they cut him up."

Kruger disappeared after a short goodbye. DeKok motioned the morgue attendants closer. With intimidated faces they looked at the mountain of flesh they were supposed to transport.

"We should have brought a wrecker, maybe even a crane," growled the older one, "What a load!"

DeKok smiled: "We'll give you a hand."

The four of them finally succeed in heaving the enormous body on the gurney. Pushing the overbalanced thing over the uneven, rotted planks of the pier to the car, was an adventure in itself. The attendants finally closed the back doors, thanked the two cops, got in front and drove away.

DeKok stared after them until the red tail lights disappeared around the corner.

* * *

As usual, at least half an hour late, DeKok stepped cheerfully into the large detective room the next day. A good night's rest had invigorated and refreshed both body and mind of the grey sleuth. He threw his hat at the peg and missed. With a boyish grin on his face he bent over and picked it up, also as usual. Then he took off his ubiquitous raincoat and ambled over toward Vledder, whose fingers were flying over the keys of an electric typewriter.

"What time is the autopsy?"

The younger man rested his fingers for a moment and looked up.

"Dr. Rusteloos called to say he would be there at ten." He looked at his watch. "I've to leave in a few minutes, or I'll be too late at the morgue."

DeKok nodded understanding.

"Watch for the bullets," he warned. "Perhaps one, or more remained stuck in all that fat. I'd like to know the caliber."

Vledder nodded absent mindedly. Then he shut off his machine and rose from his chair. A serious look on his face.

"Just seconds after nine, Commissaris Buitendam honored me with a visit." There was undeniable tension in his voice. "He asked for you."

"And?"

Vledder sighed.

"I believe he is displeased. There's a storm brewing!"

Deliberately misunderstanding, DeKok merely stared at him.

"Storm?"

Vledder nodded emphatically.

"Yes, something to do with Narcotics, as I understand it." He shook his head. "I thought they acted strangely when I inquired earlier for information about Boning and Teest. They told me that they were not giving out any information, for the time being. They treated me as if I were the press. Apparently they got a whiff of suspicion that we are meddling with "their" Ravenstein case."

DeKok partly closed his eyes.

"Who used the word 'meddle'?"

"The guys from Narcotics."

DeKok pressed his lips together. He was visibly upset. With a red face he turned and with long steps walked out of the room. Vledder ran after him, tried to stop him, but was too late.

* * *

Commissaris Buitendam, the tall, distinguished Chief of the police station at the Warmoes Street, motioned with a long, manicured, white hand. The hands always reminded DeKok of a pianist.

"Come in, DeKok," he said in his usual pompous manner, "and seat yourself." Cheerfully he came from behind his enormous desk and waved a friendly invitation toward a seating arrangement of modern furniture near the window, usually reserved for his most prominent guests. The grey sleuth pulled an unwilling face, stubborn and unapproachable. He usually rejected all attempts at cordiality from his boss. He and DeKok had co-existed in an atmosphere of barely concealed hostility for so long, it seemed natural. DeKok liked it that way. It prevented a lot of unwelcome curiosity regarding his methods of investigation.

"If it's all the same to you ... I'd rather stand."

A slight blush spread across the pale face of the commissaris.

"Please yourself."

He walked back to his desk and placed himself squarely behind it.

"You requested the files on the Ravenstein murder from Narcotics?"

"Yes."

"Why?"

"Because I have certain evidence regarding the case ... evidence which may show that the murder of Ravenstein is only marginally connected to the drug scene."

Commissaris Buitendam awarded him with a faint smile.

"The Chief of Narcotics," he said amicably, "is clearly of a different opinion."

DeKok grinned.

"Well, he's had more than a year to prove his opinion."

The commissaris waved that away.

"You know yourself," he said soothingly, "from your own experience, that investigations don't always go smoothly ... it's possible to hit all sort of snags that may delay thing."

DeKok nodded agreement.

"Certainly, but delays of more than a year are a bit excessive," he snorted. "I don't think they have made any progress at all. And I strongly suspect that this lack of progress ... the total ineffectiveness of their efforts ... are the reasons for them to withhold the files from me." The old sleuth paused. His chin jutted out and his eyes spat fire. "If they don't deliver the files to me by close of business, today, then I'll go get them in person, tomorrow! If necessary, I'll be accompanied by the new District Attorney."

With difficulty, Buitendam managed to keep his anger under control. He stretched out both hands and pressed the tips of his fingers together.

"Narcotics," he said, with a barely controlled tremor in his voice, "also wants to take over the Boning case."

Decisively DeKok shook his head.

"No way! For the time being, it is not at all certain that Boning's killing has anything to do with narcotics, that is, a drug-related crime, which may or may not be within the competence of Narcotics. And until that has been established beyond a reasonable doubt, we here, in the Warmoes Street, will maintain jurisdiction. If, after a year, I still haven't solved the case, they can have it. You understand? Then we're even."

Buitendam's face was getting dangerously red.

"According to the Chief of Narcotics, you have, without so much as a by-your-leave, messed around long enough with the Ravenstein case."

DeKok tightened his fists until the knuckles were white.

"First I have "meddled" and now "mess-ed-a-round!" he yelled angrily. "I do not *meddle*, I do not *mess-a-round*! ... I in-ves-ti-gate! And if you haven't discovered that much, after all these years, I am seriously doubting your powers of observation, minuscule as they may be!"

Enraged, Buitendam came from behind his desk, His eyes spat fire, his face was red and his nostrils trembled. He stretched an arm toward the door, like an avenging angel.

"OUT!"

DeKok left.

10

Vledder apologized wordlessly.

"I really couldn't wait any longer, this morning. I was almost too late as it was. What happened?"

"What?"

"Your interview with Buitendam."

DeKok grinned without mirth.

"As always."

"He chased you from the room?"

DeKok nodded.

"Buitendam never could control himself. He's so touchy!"

Vledder snickered: "And you're blameless!?"

DeKok pushed his lower lip forward. "Apparently the commissaris allowed himself to be influenced by the Chief of Narcotics. That worthy decided that we had already "mess-ed a-round" long enough with the Ravenstein case. I objected to the term "messing around" and I said so." The old Inspector sighed. "It isn't that I don't understand their point of view, you know, but still. The guys in Narcotics have gotten absolutely nowhere after more than a year and now they're afraid we'll solve the puzzle within the next few weeks. Doesn't make them look good."

Vledder looked mischievous: "I'd enjoy that."

DeKok ignored the remark. He could be infuriating that way.

"The Chief of Narcotics," he continued seriously, "also wanted to take over the Boning case."

Vledder looked at him wide-eyed: "I hope you refused!?"

"I told them ... after a year ... if we haven't solved it by then ... then Narcotics can have it and they can 'mess a-round' with the Boning case."

Vledder laughed.

"Messing around bothers you, doesn't it."

"Yes, it does," he answered with intensity. "I've always taken my job seriously. I'm a professional. I don't 'mess around' and I do not 'meddle.' Those terms, applied to our work, are nothing less than insulting."

He finally laid the subject to rest and changed to the daily routine.

"How was the autopsy?"

Vledder smiled.

"Even old Dr. Rusteloos was amazed. The pathologist had never, never ever in his life, cut into a corpse with such an enormous layer of fat. Unbelievable!"

"Did you see Kruger?"

Vledder nodded: "Yes, he took the prints. According to him, they have a record of a certain Arnold Boning from about seven years ago. Fraud. He was not prosecuted. Just to make sure, Ben promised to compare both sets of prints. There's a lot of 'messing around'," he winked, "with identities, these days."

"Bullets?"

Vledder searched with the tips of fingers in the breast pocket of his jacket. Produced a wad of grease paper and handed it to DeKok.

"Undamaged, well preserved, stuck in the fat ... a 7.6mm bullet!"

The old detective unwrapped the piece of paper and looked at the projectile.

"Wonderful ... all we need now is the weapon."

Vledder looked at him.

"An old Sauer, perhaps?"

DeKok smiled.

"Donkersloot is dead. But I don't suppose that Mrs. Donkersloot buried the pistol with dear Henry."

Vledder tried to move his eyebrows. As usual, he failed miserably.

"You mean, of course, that somebody else could have used the same weapon, Donkersloot's pistol?"

DeKok shrugged his shoulders.

"It's an obvious conclusion. The two murders, Ravenstein and Boning, have a lot in common ... three shots ... relatively lonely meeting place ... near water ..." He remained silent and scratched the back of his neck.

"And you know what I was wondering about, last night?"

"Well?"

"What happened to the old 7.6mm Sauer that the late Ravenstein used to own?"

Vledder gaped at him.

"Anna B-Breitenbach?" he stuttered, "w-would ... eh, would she?"

DeKok sighed.

"She certainly could, I don't know if she would, though. She knows how to handle a weapon. It's also not at all sure that her relationship with Ravenstein was as bright and sunny as she wants us to believe." He pointed his index finger at Vledder. "And she knew 'Fatman' Arnold Boning!"

"The second victim."

"Exactly!"

Vledder nodded slowly to himself.

"Anna Breitenbach," he said thoughtfully, "I hadn't thought about that. It seemed so tenuous. But, because of her relationship with Ravenstein, she most certainly was in a position to learn all about the syndicate."

DeKok grinned.

"And started a little blackmail trip on her own, stopping by one member of the syndicate after another?"

"Impossible?"

"Absolutely not!"

Giving his eyebrows up as a lost cause, Vledder wrinkled his forehead.

"Where the bullets just as nicely grouped in Ravenstein's body?"

DeKok nodded slowly.

"At the time of the first murder I already thought about an expert marksman, or woman, somebody with a lot of practice in handling a pistol. Usually the bullet wounds are more widespread and there are some misses." He leaned back in his chair, thoughtfully chewed on his lower lip. "But there are a number of things that bother me greatly," he continued, "irreconcilable things. For instance, both Boning and Ravenstein were familiar with crime, they had practically been raised in it. Experienced criminals ... part of the leadership." He spread both hands. "What sort of power does the killer have to entice them to deserted places?"

Vledder smiled.

"Our dear Anna," he said appreciatively, "is an extremely attractive young woman. For a secret rendez-vous with such a desirable creature, you wouldn't pack a gun."

DeKok looked at him with admiration.

"A very good analysis," he praised. "Love makes blind and less alert. Lust even more so." He raked fingers through his grey hair. "But we're still stuck with the confession of Donkersloot, remember him? And he supplies blackmail by Ravenstein as the motive."

Dismissing the idea as an unimportant detail, Vledder shrugged his shoulders.

"You said yourself ... Alluring Anna could easily be connected to the syndicate as a sort of *femme fatale*. Who knows, she may have had a relationship with Donkersloot as well. Perhaps that was what Ravenstein was using against old Henry."

DeKok rubbed the bridge of his nose with the tip of his pinky.

"You're in real form." he said with admiration. "Still, a relationship whereby Amazing Anna could get Donkersloot crazy enough to write a confession of the Ravenstein murder ... a murder she had committed herself?"

Vledder looked extremely self-satisfied.

"With the same old Sauer 7.6mm she had somehow obtained from him!"

Silence reigned after that. Both inspectors wrestled with their own thoughts and theories. First one possibility was scrutinized, rejected and put on hold, and then another.

Vledder finally broke the silence.

"Anna Breitenbach is an ideal suspect," he said. "And there are additional possibilities. But first, I think, we should visit her little cottage near the beach. Armed with a search warrant. Then, if we can locate the Sauer she was talking about, the one that belonged to Ravenstein, we can start comparing markings." He pointed at the bullet on DeKok's desk. "There can't be that many Sauer pistols around, I mean, do they even make them any more?"

"Yes," said DeKok, "and if the markings match, we have solved the case." He did not sound convinced.

Vledder looked at him.

"Well," he hesitated, "something still bothering you?"

DeKok did not answer at once. He moved in his chair, then leaned forward and looked earnestly at his young assistant. Carefully he began:

"I would like to accept your theory, if ... eh, if we had found Donkersloot's confession with Anna. If she had really been in possession of the confession ... But the confession was found in an old history book ... inaccessible to dear Anna, no matter how urgently she might need it. You understand, Dick, that's what makes me less than enthusiastic."

Vledder lowered his head.

"But I was so sure that we were on the right track." his tone was almost timid. "I'd hate to let go of it. Perhaps Donkersloot's nephew, Waterman, knows something about extra-marital affairs."

DeKok pointed in front of him, at nothing in particular and said sternly:

"But those affairs better be committed with charming Anna. Any other relationship, with any other woman, will not fit in with our theories." Expressionless, he looked at the young inspector and then added:

"And please keep the following maxim in mind: A blackmailer does not kill! That would be stupid. A blackmailer is very much concerned about the health and welfare of his victim. A dead victim stops payments. If a blackmail victim is killed, it will never be by the blackmailer." He remained silent for a while and then, irked, he continued: "But I don't know ... perhaps the motive in this case is blackmail after all. A blackmailer has something ... knows something ... the knowledge of something that the victim wants to keep secret ... and is prepared to pay to keep the secret. If in the case of both murders, both Ravenstein and Boning, ... if we're dealing with blackmail, we immediately are faced with the question ... what did the victim know and what did the murderer want to keep secret. In short ... who was blackmailing whom and with what?"

Vledder nodded, pretending to understand.

"Go figure!"

The grey sleuth inspected his index finger, as if wondering to what task it could be put next.

"Except for Anna, dear Anna, there is perhaps just one person left who can tell us anything."

"Teest?"

DeKok nodded.

"Bert Teest!"

There was a modest knock on the door of the detective room which immediately opened. Happily surprised the old inspector looked at the visitor. It was Jan Schouten. He waved jovially and walked rapidly toward DeKok's desk.

"Hello, it's me again."

"Yes, bookseller's son, I can see that."

Jan Schouten sank down in the chair next to the desk with easy familiarity.

"I missed the train," he panted slightly, "otherwise I would have been here at least half an hour earlier."

DeKok smiled.

"You were in a hurry?"

Jan nodded.

"Rather! Father wants me back in time for dinner."

"And at what time is that?"

"After the store closes. Father feels that the entire family should be in one place, at the same time, at least once a day. He picked dinner. He's really concerned about that." He grinned and continued: "He can also be very difficult about it. I remember once ..."

DeKok interrupted him.

"Didn't you go to Mill Lane with your father, for the books?"

Young Schouten looked at him and answered: "Yes, of course, to pick them up!"

DeKok nodded in praise.

"Exactly. Do you remember the house?"

"Of course."

"And Mrs. Donkersloot?"

Jan nodded.

"I thought she was nice. She tipped me a tenner because she thought I was working so hard."

"She's disappeared."

Jan Schouten looked surprised.

"Really?"

DeKok spread his hands.

"Nobody knows where she went and the house is empty."

"Gee!"

DeKok chuckled. The reaction from the young man was such a delightful mixture of adult understanding and boyish wonder.

"But what brought you back to Amsterdam?" he asked.

Jan smiled secretively.

"I found something else!" his voice was triumphant.

"In the book collection?" DeKok's eyebrows were poised to start their amazing gymnastics.

The boy nodded.

"I've been too busy to spend much time on it. One of the sales staff has fallen ill. I had to help out. But early this afternoon I had some time again to search through those old books."

"And?"

Jan opened his shirt.

"In a history book ... another menu from the *Poort van Eden* in Amsterdam."

Expectantly DeKok looked at the boy.

"Another confession to murder?"

Jan handed the menu to DeKok and nodded.

"The murder of Arnold Boning."

Vledder leaned forward and ripped the menu out of DeKok's hands.

"That's impossible," he cried out. "It's impossible ... im-pos-si-ble! No ... no ..."

11

DeKok looked up when Vledder came back.

"Did you get our Jan safely to the train?" he asked.

The young inspector sank panting down in a nearby chair, pulled a handkerchief from his pocket and wiped the sweat off his brow.

"It's hot outside. And the crowds! It's as if half the world has selected Amsterdam for a visit, this summer."

"Is the boy on the train?"

"Don't worry! Jan will be back in Rotterdam in plenty of time to consume the evening meal within the bosom of the family Schouten."

It sounded derisive.

DeKok pulled a serious face. He noticed the mocking tone.

"I happen to find the Central Station in Amsterdam, everything but safe," he said, visible piqued. "Especially during the summer. There is too much going on that shouldn't be allowed ... the great hall is a gathering place for all sorts of criminals and would-be criminals. I feel responsible for Jan's safety. And we *are* responsible for him. That boy comes all the way from Rotterdam in order to help us." His face became somber. "The police doesn't have that many friends left, as it is."

Vledder ignored the remarks. He was almost as accomplished at ignoring things, as was DeKok, when the mood struck him.

"Isn't it about time to confiscate the book collection of the late Sir Donkersloot?" he asked.

DeKok shook his head.

"Officially we don't have the right. We would have to obtain a court order." He shrugged his shoulders in a supremely indifferent manner. "But I don't think it's necessary. While you were taking young Jan to the train, I had a long telephone conversation with the elder Schouten. I asked him to keep the collection intact, for the time being and not to sell any of it. He promised to do so." He grinned. "And our young friend will keep searching, I think."

With a gesture of desperation, Vledder pointed at the menu on DeKok's desk.

"I hate to repeat myself, but that's impossible! That's totally impossible. Boning was killed just last night and now we have a man, who has been dead for months, confessing to the murder. Donkersloot is dead ... he couldn't be confessing to it."

DeKok picked up the menu and looked at both sides. One side was more or less normal:

Hotel-Restaurant
De Poort van Eden
Emperor's Canal
Amsterdam
Menu a la Carte

Then followed the selections and the prices. He turned

98

the menu over and looked at the handwriting on the back. With a sigh, he remarked:

"The same spidery handwriting!" he began to read:

"I, Hendrik Peter Donkersloot," read the old inspector, "hereby confess to a murder I committed. I fired with my pistol, an old Sauer 7.6mm, with malice aforethought and with full knowledge of the consequences, a total of three shots at Arnold Boning. He looked at me as if he'd seen a ghost, collapsed and was dead almost instantly. I was to meet him on Admiral's Way, behind the Central Station, at the end of Pier 27. It is a quiet spot. There I was to hand him 50,000 guilders, in bills of 100 guilders each. He was blackmailing me and because I knew there would be no end to his demands, I decided to kill him. At first I had planned to leave him there, but in order to delay the discovery of my deed, I dragged his body to the edge of the harbor and let it slip in the water. I am not sorry for what I did, but now, with the end in sight, I make this confession in order to prevent an innocent person from being charged with my crime."

DeKok threw the menu on his desk.

"You noticed something?" he asked.

Vledder moved his shoulders, as if that was obvious.

"The same text as that of the confession about Ravenstein ... and the same motive ... blackmail."

DeKok smiled as a cat that had swallowed a canary.

"Indeed, the same motive. But the text is not identical. What I noticed almost at once, is that the date and the time are missing. This confession doesn't tell us when the murder was committed. In the 'Ravenstein confession' that is exactly recorded."

He pressed his index finger against the tip of his nose.

"And something else. In the confession he writes "... I dragged his body to the edge of the harbor and let it slip in the water," but that didn't happen. Possibly because 'Fatman' was too heavy to move." He looked a question at Vledder.

"Conclusions?"

The young man hesitated.

"The confession was written before the murder was committed?"

DeKok laughed.

"Not a very intelligent remark," he said, slightly denigrating. "Of course, the confession was written before the murder. The writer was long since dead, before Boning ever met his fate."

The older man pointed at the menu and said:

"No, there is another conclusion, much more important, I think."

"Well?"

"Long-range plans had been formulated for the murder of Arnold Boning," he said formally.

"Of course, that's evident from the confession, now that you point it out. Only the time and the date weren't known at the time this was written. The place ... Pier 27 ... the weapon ... again a Sauer ... all that had been decided."

DeKok stretched a hand toward Vledder.

"But who?"

"Pardon?"

"Who are the people that made all the decisions. It couldn't have been just Donkersloot. He's dead. Somebody else had to know of the plan. Somebody had to kill Boning after Donkersloot confessed. Who else is a part of this murderous conspiracy?"

Vledder spread his arms in despair.

"Well, one of them had to be Donkersloot. He knew what was going to happen. He must have been closely connected to the planning stages." Suddenly his face lit up. "And perhaps he did it all by himself ..." Vledder paused to get the desired effect. "... alone ... without help from anyone ... there is no conspiracy ... the same man killed both Ravenstein and Boning."

DeKok pressed his lips together.

"Hendrik Peter Donkersloot is dead and buried." There was finality in his voice.

"Are you sure?"

"I have verified it with Rotterdam. I checked City Hall and asked the Rotterdam police to verify in person. All records were checked independently by at least two different sets of investigations. There is no doubt." He slapped his hands together. "The only thing we haven't done yet, is check with the doctor who signed the death certificate. Rotterdam talked to him on the phone, that's all." He smiled, "I am convinced. But if it will satisfy you, you can check the doctor out ..." He did not complete the sentence, but got up and shuffled over to the coat rack.

Vledder followed him.

"Where are you going?"

"To Edam."

"What for?"

"To tell Bert Teest that he's about to be murdered."

Vledder's mouth fell open.

"What!?"

DeKok turned around.

"I didn't stutter, nor did I speak Russian."

* * *

It took almost an hour before Vledder managed to get his new Golf untangled from city traffic. With a sigh of relief he leaned back in the seat as they turned on the A1 express way.

"It won't be long, now," he joked, "or the whole town will have a heart attack. The arteries are already clogged."

DeKok smiled faintly.

"Please, let's not have any of this kind of defeatist talk," he admonished. "According to the highest Traffic Police Authority, Amsterdam is one of the better examples of traffic management in an urban area."

Vledder snorted: "The man must be blind!"

DeKok shook his head: "No, he just wants to keep his job."

Vledder grinned and glanced briefly in DeKok's direction.

"Do you really believe that Bert Teest is about to be killed?"

DeKok scratched his neck.

"Although I am at a complete loss as to the motives, I'm afraid that Teest will indeed be the next victim. He's the last of the illustrious foursome who is still alive."

A vertical groove appeared in the middle of Vledder's forehead.

"Do you think that somebody is cheerfully trying to wipe out the entire financial backing of the Dutch drug trade?"

DeKok chuckled.

"I don't know if it's happening 'cheerfully', but it looks like that what's happening all right. I consider it a realistic possibility, anyway. Nevertheless, we have the moral duty to warn Teest."

Again Vledder snorted.

"Moral?" he asked incredulously. "Moral? What kind of moral standard are you applying, for heaven's sake?"

DeKok did not answer at once. He rubbed his eyes and thought. Then he said, slowly and hesitantly:

"I should have been more alert, right from the beginning. Much more alert. When Jan Schouten delivered the first confession, I should have asked Rotterdam to immediately confiscate the entire book collection. At the very least, I should have asked them to go through it and search it, for I know not what. But I didn't do that, because I thought we were dealing with an isolated case."

"Yes, yes," said Vledder impatiently, "the Ravenstein case."

DeKok nodded agreement, briefly laying a soothing hand on the other's shoulder.

"A murder that was more than a year old and on which Narcotics is, more than likely, completely stuck. I hoped, by means of the strange evidence, to be able to close the case quickly. That's all. I never gave the possibility of additional murders a second thought. I was really more shocked and surprised than I can tell you, when young Schouten appeared with the second confession."

"The so-called 'Boning' confession? Why?"

"What do you mean?"

"Why were you shocked and surprised?"

DeKok turned in his seat and looked at Vledder, who did not take his eyes off the road.

"If that sales assistant in Rotterdam hadn't been sick ... If young Jan had not been drafted to help out in the shop ... if he had found the second confession one day sooner ... then we could have warned Boning in time not to keep the appointment. You understand, he would still have been alive today."

Vledder shrugged his shoulders. Clearly he thought it to be an unimportant detail.

"Do you mourn his death?" He snorted contemptuously. "Do you really mourn his death? How many young people have been brought to an early grave because of his filthy trade in drugs? How many lives has he ruined? How many boys have been driven to a life of crime? How many young girls and women have been forced into prostitution? All because of that bastard!" Again he snorted with utter contempt. "You mourn his death?"

Amazed DeKok looked at his young assistant.

The violent tone, the venomous hatred, the impassioned emotions that vibrated in his every word, astonished him. The old inspector pulled on his lower lip and slowly nodded at the horizon.

"I mourn his death," he said primly, "because I could possibly have prevented it ... because of my personal negligence a human life was lost."

Vledder protested vehemently.

"You call such a big, ugly, fat parasite *human*? ... a man who earned fortunes from the misery of others!?"

DeKok sighed deeply.

"I've not been put here to judge people," he said softly. "That's not my job ... thank goodness. We've got judges and ultimately Our Dear Lord for that. I am just saddled with a conscience ... my conscience ... a conscience to which I listen as much as possible ... and a responsibility."

Not believing his ears, Vledder could not resist looking aside.

"If you had received that confession one day earlier, you would have warned Boning?"

"Absolutely!"

Vledder kept his attention on the road.

"I think," he sighed, "that I would have slept on it, for a night or two."

For several seconds DeKok looked at him, without any expression on his face. Then he tapped him lightly on the arm.

"Edam ... next right," he said.

12

"Do you know the address?"

DeKok nodded.

"According to my information, we have to be in the Rembrandt Quarter, 1138 Bredius Way."

Surprised Vledder looked at him.

"How did you get that information. The hotel register at the *Poort van Eden* listed just the name of the town, nothing more."

"The telephone, my boy, the telephone. I called the Edam police and they were most cooperative. Also, his house is hooked up to the silent alarm at the nearby station."

"What else?"

"What do you mean?"

"Did they know him?"

"As a criminal?"

"Yes."

DeKok shook his head.

"The Edam police doesn't have any damaging information about him. He's just known as a businessman. He also is not listed with the State Police. Bert Teest has no police record at all."

Vledder grinned, but the laughter did not reach his eyes.

"And if we can believe our dear Anna," he said with a considerable amount of emotion, "Bert Teest is a pitiless brute, one who doesn't hesitate to take whatever violent steps are necessary. A man, according to her dear, departed 'Friedreich *von* Ravenstein' with a record a mile long, despite his relatively young age."

DeKok made a nonchalant gesture.

"But why not? Some criminals have developed a special instinct that helps keep them out of the hands of the police. I could introduce you to a few that have lived off crime, practically since the day they were born, and have never even seen the inside of a police station."

"And Teest is such a person?"

"Perhaps." He shrugged his shoulders. "If that's so, it means that Teest is an extremely shrewd and intelligent person and we should approach him with care."

"And that's the sort of man who, according to your 'moral' duty, should be warned about his upcoming assassination?" grinned Vledder. The tone of voice was mocking and unbelieving.

DeKok maintained an expressionless face. It wasn't at all difficult for him to ignore the implied ridicule.

"Certainly," he said slowly, "that's a moral obligation I cannot ignore."

Vledder tried again.

"Do you remember that Ravenstein said something along the lines of if-something-ever-happens-to-me-then-I-will-not- be-his-first-victim?"

"Yes, I remember," DeKok nodded, resigned.

Vledder would not be denied.

"Then, what, in the name of sanity, are we doing here?" His emotions threatened to get the better of him. He went on: "So, if something happens to Bert Teest, it's no more than just ... no more than he deserves!"

DeKok looked at his young colleague with a pained expression on his face.

"You're so emotional ... so rebellious."

Vledder pressed his jaws tightly shut.

"I'm not emotional, or rebellious," he said finally, just as emotional as before. "I'm just angry. Why do we bother? If the drug king pins want to liquidate each other, that's fine with me ... that can only benefit society. Do we have to prevent it? ... Do we have to warn a man like that, that his murderer is waiting for him? He probably knows that better than we do!"

DeKok smiled sadly.

"The warning," he answered mysteriously, "is not the only reason for which we've come to Edam. What do you think of the possibility that Bert Teest might have gotten the idea that it would be nice if the enormous profits, which the syndicate undoubtedly made, didn't have to be shared any longer?"

Vledder's eyes suddenly widened. The Golf crossed the center line, but he quickly corrected the aberration in his driving. Enthusiastically he exclaimed:

"That's it! That's it ... the motive for the killings of Ravenstein and Boning! Shrewd little Bert fixed them. He's all set now. He's obtained his goal. Completely. The others are dead. He doesn't have to share anymore! He can keep all the profits for himself!" He slapped his hand against his forehead. "How stupid of me, not to have realized that sooner!"

DeKok merely glanced at him and did not react.

The Bredius Way turned out to be a wide lane with mighty chestnut trees on both sides of the street and expensive villas, partly hidden by the luxurious growth of plants, bushes and other trees.

On the side of a driveway, flanked with high, purple rhododendrons that wafted their sweet smelling aroma through the soft summer air, half hidden among the greenery, Vledder discovered a granite capped, brick pillar with the number 1138 in elegant bronze.

The young inspector stopped the car and pointed at the driveway.

"What do you think, park here, or drive in? The car, at least, will not put us to shame in such surroundings."

DeKok laughed.

"You and your new car," he said. Then: "Drive on!"

The gravel in the driveway crunched underneath the radial tires of the new Golf. They parked behind a red Mitsubishi Starion, almost in front of the wide steps leading to the double, oak front door. Slowly they emerged from the car and slowly they walked toward the front door. In front of the door, DeKok stopped and asked: "Do you see a name, anywhere?"

"No, just a bell." Vledder pointed at a button, to the left of the door.

DeKok pressed the button and they could just hear, somewhere within the bowels of the large house, the sound of a subdued "ding-dong". Then the heavy door was opened by a young, blonde woman. DeKok estimated her to be in her early twenties. She wore a short, tight, black dress and a minuscule white apron. With a questioning look in her eyes she looked at the two detectives. The grey sleuth politely lifted his little hat and made a slight bow.

"My name is DeKok," he said, friendly, "with ... eh, Kay-Oh-Kay." He pointed to the side. "And this is my colleague Vledder. We're inspectors of the Amsterdam Police and would like to talk to Mr. Teest."

The face of the young woman fell.

"I don't know if Mr. Teest will receive you."

DeKok nodded encouragement at her.

"Just try," he said in his most winning tone of voice. "Just tell Mr. Teest that it's a matter of life, or death, and we do not intend to return."

The young woman opened the door wider, let the two visitors enter and led them to large side room.

"Wait here," she commanded decisively. "I'll ask Mr. Teest if he can spare the time to see you."

With attractively swinging hips she walked away from them, down the long, wide corridor. DeKok looked after her and could not resist to ask himself naughtily what exactly her function might be in the villa. She returned after a few minutes and beckoned.

"Follow me."

She swayed away in front of them. About halfway down the corridor she stopped and with an inviting gesture opened the door of a large room. DeKok and Vledder stepped inside. The room was almost exactly square with heavy beams supporting the ceiling. Around a stylish open hearth built of sepia colored flagstone, stood a group of four heavy, leather arm chairs. A broad shouldered man, dressed in a deep blue robe, was seated in the extreme left of the chairs. With a broad smile on his face he rose and approached DeKok. "What honor ... such an honor," he cried with false gaiety. "A great sleuth in my humble abode. Welcome!"

The "great" sleuth gave him a penetrating look. He estimated the man to be in his middle thirties. He had a full, somewhat puffed face and dark, slicked down hair, gleaming with hair oil. His light brown eyes were alert. After having shaken both detectives by the hand, he made an expansive gesture toward the easy chairs.

"Take a seat ... take a seat," he said jovially. "Can I offer the gentlemen a drink?"

DeKok looked at his watch and noticed sadly that a visit to the small bar of Little Lowee would be out of the question for today.

"A cognac, please."

Bert Teest smiled. "Your favorite beverage, I read that somewhere." He looked at Vledder: "The same?"

The young inspector nodded. Teest walked to the door, yelled some instructions down the hall, came back and took a seat opposite DeKok.

"A matter of life, or death?" he asked with a smile.

The old inspector placed his hat on the floor, next to the chair, and reviewed his answer. Then he began carefully:

"I will begin by telling you what we know and I am not naive enough to expect you to confirm my story." He paused, stretched his hands out in front of him and pressed the tips of his fingers together. "Messrs. Donkersloot, Ravenstein, Boning and yourself formed a syndicate to finance the drug traffic. As far as we know, Donkersloot died a natural death, but Ravenstein and Boning were killed in an almost identical manner. We expect that you will receive a request, one of these days, to keep an appointment, or meet someone, in a deserted location. I advise you not to keep such a meeting, but instead, to immediately notify me when you receive such a request. Tell me exactly the time, the date and the place of the meeting. I will then be able to take certain measures. After all, I am very curious to discover the identity of the man, or the woman, behind all this."

Teest nodded understanding.

"That would then be the man, or woman, responsible for the killing of Ravenstein and Boning."

DeKok cocked his head.

"You know both gentlemen?"

Teest smiled sardonically.

"I knew them, yes."

"And Donkersloot?"

"A nice man ... at first glance," nodded Teest.

DeKok listened to the tone in which Test spoke.

"Bad experiences with Donkersloot?"

Teest shook his head.

"No comment ... also no comment regarding the nature of my relationship with the gentlemen you named. You understand."

"And my request?"

Teest did not answer. The door opened and the young woman entered, carrying a tray with a bottle of Remy Martin and three large snifters. The liquid was poured out with a gurgling sound, she handed each of them a glass and disappeared. DeKok warmed the glass in his hands.

"My request?" he repeated.

Teest took a sip of cognac.

"What could be the consequences for me?" he asked.

DeKok smiled ironically.

"You would be assisting the police to apprehend the man, or woman, who also plans to kill you."

Teest shook his head, annoyed.

"That's not what I mean. Suppose that with my cooperation, you catch the murderer, or murderess, of Ravenstein and Boning. Then he, or she, makes some heavily damaging statements to you about me ... something that may force you take official steps against me. Unless ..." He did not finish the sentence, but allowed DeKok a look at his greasy smile.

"Unless what?"

Teest gestured vaguely, hesitated a moment and said:

"I deliver a murderer, or murderess ... and I can count on your silence."

DeKok rubbed the back of his nose with the tip of his pinky.

"Is such a thing possible?"

"What do you mean?"

"That the murderer, or murderess, can make heavily damaging statements against you?"

Bert Teest shrugged his shoulders. He seemed unconcerned.

"Well, if somebody has conceived the idea to kill me, then, I assume ... he, or she, must have sufficient reasons to do so ... although I cannot possibly imagine what those reasons could be." He remained silent for a while, leaned back in his chair and then, after another sip of his cognac, continued: "But, for a great and respected sleuth, you are this time on the wrong trail. My life is not at all in any danger, whatsoever."

DeKok closed his eyes half way and studied the puffy face of the other.

"You're sure of that?"

Teest nodded convincingly.

"The motive, origin, reason, call it what you will, for the murders is not to be found in the alleged drug traffic ... or the alleged financing of such alleged drug traffic ... it has nothing to do with that."

DeKok grinned.

"And ... because the murders have nothing to do with the ... eh, drug traffic, or the financing thereof, your life is not in danger?"

Teest shook his head and sighed.

"I am just trying to place myself in your situation. You start by assuming there is indeed a syndicate, engaged in the financing of an extensive drug network. Of the members of this assumed, and alleged, syndicate, I am the last living survivor. Therefore you fear that I may be killed as well and you ask my cooperation in apprehending and arresting the alleged killer."

He shook his head again and pointed at DeKok. Then he said:

"No, no, the person who killed Ravenstein and Boning, doesn't need me as a victim. She has obtained her objective."

The old inspector leaned forward.

"*Her* objective?" he asked, shocked.

Bert Teest merely nodded.

"Anna Breitenbach ... for the last five, or six years she's been having an affair with Peter Valenkamp, manager of the *Poort van Eden.*

13

Bert Teest walked them to the door. He kept the heavy oak door open and waved goodbye. Friendly, even jovial. But there was a secretive grin on his weak, slightly puffy face, as if he had just achieved a personal triumph.

The two detectives shuffled back to the car. Before getting in, DeKok turned once more and looked at the silhouette of the man in the door. A broad shouldered Bert Teest. He wondered what the future would bring ... if their paths would cross again ... and under what circumstances.

Vledder turned the car in the driveway and drove to the street. It was dark on Bredius Way. High above, above the dense foliage of the trees, they saw some stray rays of moonlight.

They drove on in silence. At first Vledder stopped for a red light at the end of the road, but when he saw no other traffic, he moved on and made a right turn. DeKok saw it. He wanted to say something, but restrained himself. How many times, he thought, did people run a red light? Too often, he thought, much too often. And who could catch them all. Who would watch the crossings, in traffic, as well as in life. Who made sure that everybody obeyed the rules? Police? There weren't enough police, not nearly enough police ... and there were too many crossings and intersections. He smiled. His thoughts amused him.

Not until they had reached the A1 again, aimed at Amsterdam, did Vledder break the silence. He glanced briefly at DeKok who was struggling with his seat belts. The old inspector found it difficult to adjust to the shoulder harness. He felt constricted.

"What do you think?"

DeKok looked up.

"About what?"

"The idea that Anna Breitenbach should be responsible for two murders?"

"We've considered it before, you and I," he growled.

"Yes, well?"

"There was never an acceptable motive."

Vledder suddenly became enthusiastic. He shouted:

"But now we have a motive! An excellent motive, I think. Just think! Beautiful, young, energetic Anna Breitenbach, full of life, lives together with old, stuffy, reserved, Frederik Ravenstein. But at the same time she has an affair, an intimate affair, with Peter Valenkamp, manager, ambitious, who would love to own, or start, his own hotel. Anna gets old Fred crazy enough that he settles a nice little cottage on her, in addition to an adequate income. She's so overcome with gratitude that she uses Fred's own pistol, the old Sauer, to send him to another world. The next obstacle is 'Fatman' Arnold Boning, a man, as we have been able to observe ourselves, who is totally despised and envied by dear Anna's boyfriend, the forenamed Valenkamp. Anna entices Boning to meet her at the end of deserted Pier Numero 27, near the harbor and rewards him with three bullets from the same old Sauer, so conveniently provided by the late Fred! Peter Valenkamp is now free to pursue his dream of taking over the so much desired *Poort van Eden* and they live happily ever after."

DeKok chuckled: "Beautiful. Beautiful!" he almost sang the words. "So beautiful and so logically and cynically put together! I didn't think you had it in you!"

It sounded too enthusiastic. Vledder noticed that all right. He looked suspiciously at his older colleague.

"No good?" he asked, beginning to doubt. "Something wrong? You don't believe the possibilities forwarded by Teest?"

DeKok pursed his lips. Slowly and thoughtfully he answered:

"Oh, it's a real nice theory. It could ... even a public prosecutor could ...eh, be convinced. Perhaps there's a grain of truth in it, somewhere." He pulled a worried face. "But we must keep in mind, that the germ for the idea originates with Bert Teest ... a man who saw his amorous pursuit of Anna nipped in the bud and, perhaps, he's now just out for revenge."

"Teest is that kind of man?"

DeKok appeared thoroughly irked. His tone was sharp, when he answered.

"That's the second time you have posed that kind of question. I can't judge what sort of man he is. This was the first and only time I've ever even met Teest." He paused. "But as far as women are concerned, I do believe that he's the kind of man that would try to wink at the nurse in the hospital, when she came to cover his face prior to shipping him to the morgue. All right?"

It was Vledder's turn to laugh.

"Well, he did admit that he had been pursuing beautiful Anna for some time and had tried just about everything to convince her. Without success, of course."

119

"And that was the total extent of his confessions, by the way. A confession that didn't hurt him at all, at all. He categorically denied any threats against Ravenstein, because of Anna, or otherwise. If Anna said that, he said as if butter wouldn't melt in his mouth, she must have simply misunderstood me. He kept completely aloof and remained non-committal throughout. I was frankly surprised that he admitted having been to the *Poort van Eden* and that he knew Messrs Boning, Donkersloot and Ravenstein, however slightly. Not a word about drugs and he also completely denied any business relationship with the other three." The inspector pushed his lower lip forward. "A shrewd man, Bert Teest, yes he is. Also an extremely dangerous opponent, I think."

Vledder kept his eyes on the road and did not answer. It was as if he had not been listening ... as if the words of his older colleague had not been absorbed. Suddenly he slowed the Golf down and took the next exit.

Surprised, DeKok looked at him and asked:

"What are you doing?"

"We're going back."

DeKok's eyebrows started to vibrate, as if in preparation for one of their famous ripples.

"Back to Edam ... to Teest?"

"No, to the beach."

DeKok grimaced.

"The beach?"

"Yes, the beach, near Seadike, the cottage of Anna Breitenbach!"

"But why?"

"To see if she's still got the late Ravenstein's pistol."

"The Sauer, 7.6mm?"

"What else?"

"Do you have a search warrant?" DeKok asked, startled.

"No, of course not," answered Vledder casually. "Why should I ... don't you have your little instrument?"

Vledder brought the new Golf back onto the A1. The traffic, all leaving the city, was almost as bad as it had been in the heart of town. With one difference. Everybody went into the same direction and at breakneck speed. Surprised, DeKok looked at the speedometer and then at the traffic, back again to the speedometer. After a while he said:

"What happened to the speed limit?"

"Hey," Vledder said, "you got to match your speed to the flow of traffic and most of them think that this is just another 'Autobahn'. But you're right. We're not in Germany. However, there seems to be no effective way to enforce the speed limits."

"Well," said DeKok, "after all, you run red lights."

Vledder snorted.

"Traffic lights are invented to regulate the flow of traffic ... and when there is no traffic ..."

"... then you feel obliged to ignore them," completed DeKok.

"Exactly."

The old inspector shook his head in disapproval, but let it be. The puritan soul of DeKok constantly had difficulties adjusting to a modern, fast-paced, computer-oriented society. He felt, not for the first time, that he had been born at least one hundred years too late. He belonged in the time of the stage coach, the carrier pigeon, the Erie canal and leisurely trips on comfortable barges. When people took the time to smoke from long-stemmed porcelain pipes. Pipes that forced one to be calm and careful, because any unexpected movement might break them.

Vledder turned off the A1 at the Seadike exit. He was familiar with the area. It had been a favorite vacation spot in his youth. Expertly he used every possible shortcut. They were heading for the curiously named Sheep Drift. Unlike so many of these names in the newer developments, this particular area had indeed been a gathering point for sheep herders, clippers and traders some six or seven hundred years ago.

DeKok broke the silence with a question.

"What's the plan, if she's home?"

"Ring the bell," Vledder said casually.

DeKok rubbed his nose.

"And then we just ask if she wouldn't mind giving us the old Sauer pistol? You know, madam, the one used to kill Ravenstein and Boning. Do you mind?" His voice dripped with sarcasm.

Vledder shook his head. Calmly he said:

"Oh, I think we can manage to be just a little more subtle than all that. She told us herself that Ravenstein used to own a Sauer. We can just ask her what happened to it after his death."

"Oh, sure, we can ask her," agreed DeKok, nodding in confirmation, "but do you really think she'll run to show us the place where it's hidden? I mean ... just in case dear Anna really did away with the two men."

Vledder sighed in exasperation.

"Maybe she's not even at home ... maybe she's in Amsterdam with her boyfriend in the *Poort van Eden* ... you just apply the little invention of Handy Henkie, we go inside and look at leisure. Nobody the wiser."

"Optimist," laughed DeKok. Then he turned toward his partner, changed his tone and said earnestly: "Don't you think it might be a good idea to check first if there's indeed an affair between Anna and Valenkamp? Just think ... if there is no such relationship, the motive is gone and with that, the convenient theory of Brother Teest."

"We're almost there," growled Vledder. Then, almost pleading: "Why not try it? After all, it's just possible we will find the Sauer and then we can test the markings and if they match the bullets found in Ravenstein, or Boning, or both, we're done.. Come on, it's worth a try!? We'll have solved the case!"

"And amorous Anna will be the multiple killer."

"Yes."

DeKok looked ahead and remained silent. He didn't want to discourage his young colleague any further. But he was not convinced at all. As Vledder turned into the Sheep Drift, DeKok also recognized the area, but he could not remember what particular murder case had brought him here before. Vledder stopped the car and pointed through the windshield.

"It's the next house. Do you have your handy-dandy tool ready?"

DeKok grinned.

"Always. Ever since my friend Handy Henkie, the burglar, went straight, I've been using it in crooked ways."

"Mis-used, you mean."

Softly they approached the cottage, which turned out to be a medium-sized villa. Definitely a far cry from the "cottage" they had envisioned. The sound of the distant sea, breaking against the basalt of the nearby Seadike, was briefly overwhelmed by a heartrending screech. Momentarily petrified, they stopped. A big, black tomcat, all abristle and with a fat tail, disappeared into the bushes on the side of the house.

DeKok grinned, embarrassed.

"A bad sign," he murmured.

They could just decipher "F. Ravenstein" in faded letters on the mail box, attached to the half-open gate. They entered and proceeded along the garden path. Gravel crunched underfoot. The villa seemed deserted. There was no sign of life. Everything was dark.

Carefully they approached the green lacquered front door between two tall conifers. DeKok produced the narrow brass tube with the telescoping and adjustable skeleton keys. As he bend down to take a closer look at the type of lock he would have to adjust for, he noticed much to his surprise, that the front door was unlocked and open. It was a narrow gap, but the door was definitely not closed. The old inspector placed a shoulder against the door and pushed slowly. The door opened wider. Slowly he pushed it all the way open.

Vledder panted on his heels.

"Somebody inside?" he whispered.

DeKok did not answer. Carefully he walked inside. He put Handy Henkie's little gadget back in his trouser pocket, took a firmer grip on the flashlight and sent an oval circle of light dancing in front of them. Past a glass inner door, they reached the hall. Vledder stood next to him.

"Somebody inside?" he whispered again.

The old sleuth shrugged his shoulders. Suddenly, in the reflected light of the flashlight he noticed the weapon in the hand of his younger colleague. He tapped his index finger on the barrel.

"Put that thing away," he hissed, "before somebody gets hurt."

With obvious reluctance, Vledder complied.

Behind a door on the left, they heard a soft, unidentifiable sound. DeKok immediately flicked the flashlight off. On tiptoe they crept forward and placed themselves, one on either side, next to the door.

Long seconds went by and then the door opened. A person shuffled past them, into the hall.

With a quick grab, Vledder took the figure by the shoulder and pressed the left arm up and behind the back. A cry of fear and pain sounded in the dark.

DeKok flicked his flashlight back on and aimed the beam into the surprised face of a young man. The inspector estimated him to be about twenty five years of age. He had a long, oval face, blue eyes and short hair, almost a crew-cut. A crowbar fell from his right hand and clattered on the marble floor tiles of the hall.

DeKok came closer.

"Who are you?" he asked sternly.

For a moment the young man hesitated.

"Erik ... Erik Ravenstein."

"What are you doing here?"

A bitter smile marred the oval face of the young man.

"Looking ... looking for my father's money."

14

DeKok picked up the crowbar and gave Vledder a sign to release Erik Ravenstein. He looked at the hands of the young man and then let his gaze glide upward. There was a broad grin on his face.

"You ever heard of fingerprints?" he asked sarcastically. "Probably not, eh? Didn't you know that it is the custom to wear gloves when breaking and entering? If not, you will leave your calling card behind. Ev-e-ry-time."

Erik Ravenstein hung his head.

"I'm no burglar," he said stubbornly. "I've done nothing wrong."

DeKok pretended amazement. He lifted the crowbar. "How do you want me to explain your presence here, accompanied by this rather esoteric hunk of iron?"

Erik Ravenstein gestured vaguely.

"I ...eh, I ..."

It was the limit of his utterance.

DeKok pointed over his shoulder: "What have you touched, inside?"

Erik shook his head.

"Nothing, not yet. The bitch has moved all the furniture around." He pointed ahead: "My father's desk used to be in that room, there, with a large steel cash-box in the lower right hand drawer. He used to keep his important papers in it. It's in the bedroom now."

DeKok ignored the remark and cocked his head.

"Bitch?" he asked. "Is there a dog here?" Feigning bewilderment, he continued: "What bitch are you talking about?"

Young Ravenstein threw his head back: "The bitch, the one that was shacked up here with my father?"

"Ah, you mean Anna Breitenbach?"

Erik nodded: "That's her name all right. Anna, Anna Breitenbach. I've been following her for weeks. Thursday's, I've found out, she's always in Amsterdam, at the *Poort van Eden*. She's got something on with a man who works there."

DeKok gestured with the crowbar: "And it's Thursday, today?"

A fleeting smile flashed on the young man's face.

"That's why I came tonight. Of course, I hadn't taken you into account." He looked around. "Did she have a silent alarm, or something?"

DeKok did not answer. He did not find the young man unsympathetic. On the contrary. His almost naive frankness touched him.

"How did you get in?"

"With the key."

"You had a key?"

Erik Ravenstein nodded emphatically. "Oh, yes, we've always had a key. We used to come here for vacation, ... mother, my younger brother and I, ... when, ...eh, when father was still acting normal."

"When, eh?" asked DeKok. Then, slowly: "When did he become abnormal?"

Erik shrugged his shoulders: "Suddenly ... he suddenly started to bring all sorts of young chicks home with him ... always different ... they would stay supposedly for a visit, but father would sleep with them. If mother said anything about it, he would laugh at her. It was an impossible situation. Finally mother gave him an ultimatum: either the girl friends left, or we would leave."

DeKok nodded understanding. "So you moved out," he concluded with a sigh. The old Inspector stuck out his hand. "The key," he said, "I want the key to this house."

Ravenstein felt in his pants pockets and produced the key.

"Do you have any spares? At home?"

"No, this is the only one, it was overlooked."

"Does your mother know you're here?"

Young Erik shook his head: "I did it all on my own initiative. Mother would never have approved."

DeKok nodded to himself and waved toward the door. "Let's go."

After they had all left, the old man used Erik's key to carefully lock the front door and then he put the key in his pocket.

With the young man between them they walked across the quiet Sheep Drift toward the car. The pale moonlight threw elongated shadows on the pavement before them.

DeKok told Erik to sit in the back. He then got in himself and indicated to Vledder that he was ready to leave. The young man leaned forward.

"What are you going to do with me?" There was fear and uncertainty in his voice.

DeKok half turned in his seat: "I have to think about that." He was silent. "You said," he continued after a while, "that you were looking for your father's money?"

"Yes," nodded Erik. "When father was still alive he used to send us an allowance every month. It was enough. It was more than we needed. After he was murdered, the payments stopped and we haven't received a penny since. That's more than a year ago. Mother had saved a little, not much, but enough for about a year. We're very careful. I've a reasonably good job, not too bad a salary, but my younger brother is still in college. It costs."

DeKok showed his astonishment: "But didn't you, during all that time, take any action to recover your father's money?"

Young Ravenstein nodded: "Of course. After my father's death, mother has been here several times to talk to that bitch. But the damn bitch says there's no money left ... that she's unable, financially, to continue the allowance! We found a lawyer. It appeared that father didn't leave a will. But one way, or the other, that bitch has managed to get the villa in her own name and, according to the lawyer, there's no money under my father's name in any bank." The young man gestured wildly. "And that's impossible! Father was a wealthy man."

DeKok rubbed the back of his neck: "So, you think that ... eh, Miss Breitenbach has, in some way, managed to empty your father's bank accounts in favor of herself?" He continued: "Among ourselves let's just refer to her as Anna Breitenbach, all right? The word 'bitch' always makes me think of kennels, you know."

"OK," said Erik, resigned. "Anna Breitenbach. At home we always refer to her as 'that bitch', therefore ..."

DeKok smiled.

"I understand," he said. He looked at the young man with a friendly face: "I asked you a question."

Erik Ravenstein nodded: "I know, you want to know if I think she's transferred my father's money under her own name, into her own account."

"Exactly."

Young Erik made a helpless gesture: "That ... eh, that, I mean Anna showed mother once the amounts of money she used to get from father on a regular basis, as presents, or as an allowance. Altogether it was a small fortune. But, when compared to father's total assets, a small percentage. She may have invested it carefully. It's also possible that she has bank accounts, full of father's money in foreign countries, countries with secret bank numbers. Who knows. That's almost impossible to find out. According to our lawyer, we'll never find out."

DeKok snorted.

"And then you though: 'Come, let's take a look in the villa. Perhaps we can discover if Anna has such a foreign bank account.' Perhaps you thought to find some papers, or letters?"

"Exactly. With that kind of proof I would have been able ... with help from the lawyer ... to, eh, to put some force behind our demands. Father's money must have gone somewhere, after all. It couldn't possibly have been spent. Not *all* of it! Not even by ... eh, by such an expensive eh, ... lady, as Miss Breitenbach."

For a moment the young man sank back into the pristine back seat of the new Golf, but almost immediately he leaned forward again.

"Have you thought about what you're going to do with me?" his tone was anxious.

DeKok shrugged: "What does the police usually do with people they find in somebody else's home?"

"They lock 'em up?"

DeKok grinned: "If there's room. Nowadays that can cause certain problems." The old Inspector took a deep breath, sighed, and continued: "But that's not my concern, right now. You still live at home? With your mother?"

"Yes."

"Where?"

"In Amsterdam, the Churchill Lane."

DeKok pointed at the young man: "We'll take you home."

Erik looked at him suspiciously: "And then?" he asked.

DeKok spread his hands.

"Then nothing. You and I forget we've seen each other tonight."

A shy smile played around Erik's lips. "Is that possible?" he asked.

DeKok nodded vaguely. "Sure," he said carelessly. "My colleague, too, can be as silent as the grave. It's part of the job." The older detective plucked thoughtfully at his lower lip. "Do you plan to carry on?"

"With what?"

"Following Anna Breitenbach."

Erik nodded: "Yes," he said, "it's the only way I know to ... the only chance to ... eh, maybe, to find out something about my father's money."

"And to whom do you report? I mean, who else knows that you're following Anna Breitenbach? Who knows what you see and hear?"

"Nobody."

DeKok looked at him.

"Suppose you told me, or my colleague. You can always find us through the station in the Warmoes Street."

"You're interested?"

DeKok smiled a sardonic smile.

"Extremely," he said.

* * *

After they had dropped Erik off near his home, Vledder steered the car toward the Apollo Lane. He looked aside:

"Was it wise to make that agreement with the boy?"

DeKok shrugged.

"What else is left? I could hardly arrest him for breaking and entering. We would have had to turn him over to the local police. Then what? Our own position was difficult to explain. How were we to justify our presence in Anna's house? We just happened to pass by ... we just happened to notice the open door and we just happened to find Erik?"

"That happens to be at least one coincidence too many," grinned Vledder.

DeKok slid down in the seat.

"Besides, Erik is definitely not a burglar. He was just checking on the inheritance supposedly left by his father."

"A lot of money, earned by crime."

"That's not the boy's fault," DeKok shook his head. "It may be possible that Erik and his family don't even know how Ravenstein gained his fortune."

Vledder slapped the steering wheel with a petulant gesture.

"You gotta admit, it's strange. All that money gone ... without a trace ... and not a penny for the wife and children."

DeKok nodded, deep in thought. Then he said:

"We'll have to check if Alfred Boning left anything, or if he also, was almost bankrupt when he died."

Vledder look at him, surprised.

"Perhaps there's a motive connected to that," he cried enthusiastically.

DeKok ignored both the remark and the enthusiasm. He looked at the traffic around him.

"Where are you going?"

"I'm taking you home."

DeKok shook his head decisively.

"No," he said. "No, we're first heading back to the barn. We've been gone for quite a while. Perhaps there are new developments."

Vledder looked chagrined.

"It's almost eleven. Just for once, I would like to get a good night's sleep."

"Tomorrow."

The young Inspector sputtered some, but took the next turn-off and headed back toward the station. It was still busy in the old center of Amsterdam. The terraces were still overflowing. The balmy night lured people outside. They parked the car in the lot and strolled toward the front of the building. The doors of all the bars in the street were opened wide and here too, the terraces were full. Fragments of music, from a dozen different melodies, mingled with a constant buzz of conversation, the occasional yell, or raucous laughter.

As soon as they entered the lobby, the desk sergeant, Kusters, motioned them closer. DeKok approached.

"Something up?"

The sergeant pointed upstairs.

"There's a young lady waiting for you upstairs. She's been there more than an hour already. I was just going to send her home, but I called your wife first and she said you weren't home yet."

DeKok smiled.

"And then you thought I might just stop by the barn, before going home?"

"I know you," grinned Kusters.

"Did she leave a name?"

The sergeant shook his head.

"I didn't bother to ask her name. She was very nervous. I tried to stall her, to change her mind ... to get her to come back tomorrow, but she was going to wait for you, no matter what."

DeKok turned and started to climb the stairs to the third floor. Vledder followed. A young, blonde woman was waiting on the bench, just outside the large detective room. As soon as she saw DeKok, she ran toward him, wild, abandoned, with a teary face.

"You must stop him," she cried desperately. "You must stop him, before it's too late!"

DeKok looked momentarily confused. Then he recognized the blonde who, earlier that night, had opened the door for them in Edam. She had been dressed in a short, black, tight dress with a small, white apron.

"Who must be stopped?" he asked calmly, but still confused.

She grabbed the lapels of his raincoat.

"Bert ... Bert Teest. He's gone ... he's gone to get himself killed!"

15

DeKok pulled a face. "Gone ... to get himself killed?" he repeated.

The young woman nodded emphatically.

"He took his pistol," she said.

"Why?" he asked sternly. "To be killed, or ... to kill someone?"

The young woman looked at him with scared, teary eyes, but did not answer. DeKok took her by the arm and felt her body shake with emotion. He turned her gently in the direction of the detective room, where he placed her on the chair next to his desk.

Vledder came with a glass of water. She accepted it with shaking hands and took a few sips. Her teeth rattled against the glass. DeKok let her be for a while ... waited patiently for her to regain he composure.

"What's you name?" he asked kindly.

She placed the half full glass on the edge of the desk.

"Agatha, ... Agatha Aleph. They call me Aggie."

"And what is your relationship with Bert Teest?"

"I'm his girl friend ... have been, for the last two years, at least. But Bert doesn't want anybody to know that we're involved."

"Why not?"

"He'd lose face."

DeKok looked at her with genuine amazement.

"He'd lose face?" He repeated, disbelieving.

Aggie nodded.

"That's what he says."

DeKok snorted contemptuously. "That's why you're walking around like a lascivious French maid in a cheap movie?" His tone was no longer friendly.

Aggie lowered her head.

"I don't like it either, but that's what Bert wants. If there are any visitors I have to put that idiotic apron on. And I always have to be dressed in black."

"Like tonight?"

Again the blonde head bobbed up and down. "Like tonight," she repeated evenly. "I was really scared when you identified yourselves as police inspectors."

"Why?"

Agatha Aleph sighed deeply, followed by a shudder and some suppressed sobs.

"I'm always afraid that he'll be arrested, one of these days."

DeKok acted as if he did not understand her.

"Has he done anything ... committed murder ... or what?"

"I just have a feeling that Bert is involved in a lot of unsavory business."

"Like what?"

The woman shook her head.

"I'd rather not talk about it. I'm not sure, anyway. Bert never talks about it. Also, I'm not here to file a complaint against him. You can't expect that from me. I'm his girl fiend ... I love him, despite his sometimes rough manners."

DeKok looked serious.

"And you're afraid that something will happen to him?"

Agatha closed both eyes momentarily.

"You may not understand, but for months now, I have been possessed by a nameless fear ... every moment of the day or the night ... I expect something to happen. Something bad. That's why I was so curious tonight ... I wanted to know why you were there. That's why I was listening at the door."

DeKok shook his head, censuring her with his glance.

"That's not very nice."

Aggie shrugged her shoulders carelessly.

"I was able to follow the conversation, between you and Bert, almost word for word."

DeKok's eyebrows started their amazing dance.

"Then you must have heard that I expected him to get a call, one of these days, for a meeting in some deserted spot ... and that I advised him not to accede to such a request."

The woman swallowed.

"That's right. And I also know that he won't listen to you. I know him too well for that. He's going to go .... alone ... take care of his own business, himself ... as always."

DeKok looked thoughtful.

"That's rather dangerous in this case."

"That's exactly what I told him, after you two left," she nodded in agreement with her own words. "I told him in no uncertain terms. After all, I'm not crazy. I *know* what happened to Ravenstein and Boning."

"Well, and?"

"Bert didn't want to listen! He told me that Fred and Arnold had been killed because of motives that simply didn't apply to him. That's why I didn't have to worry that something was going to happen to him. I told him he was a liar ... I didn't believe him. When he started to laugh I couldn't stop myself. I told him I had listened to the whole thing through the door. And furthermore ... I was convinced that you were right and that he was in grave danger. The same danger that put an end to his cohorts."

DeKok listened carefully to the emotional outburst.

"What did Bert do, then?"

"He became very angry. Cursed me for a spy and a slut ... he called me just about everything you can think of. He was beside himself. He grabbed me by the wrists and dragged me out of the room and locked me into the bedroom." She showed her wrists and smiled sadly at the Inspector. She sighed. "He's done that before. Then he made a few short phone calls. I could hear him. I listened at the door of the bedroom and I heard him walk across the hall. He went to the cupboard where he keeps his pistol. Then I heard him walk out and I heard the front door slam behind him. I opened the bedroom window and lowered myself to the garden below. I ran after him, but," despondently she shook her head, "but I was too late. He was already in the car."

Aggie remained silent after that. For measurable minutes she looked, almost dazed, at the floor. Obviously she was reliving the events of the last few hours.

DeKok looked at her profile ... the line from forehead, nose and chin. She wasn't at all ugly, he concluded. On the contrary. Her long blonde hair reminded him of the bewitching Anna Breitenbach. A smile briefly displaced the lips of the old Inspector. He could appreciate Bert's taste in women.

"I've got a small car," Aggie suddenly continued. "A Fiat Ritmo. It's usually parked on the side of the house. I got in and tried to follow him, but he was out of sight after just a few hundred meters. His Mitsubishi is fast."

DeKok rubbed the back of his neck. It was a gesture of complete weariness.

"Any idea where he might have gone?"

Aggie shook her head.

"No," she answered sadly, "not the slightest idea. But I think that Bert knew exactly what appointment, ...eh, meeting you were talking about ... he'd received a request for just such a meeting a few days ago."

* * *

DeKok had tired feet. With his trouser legs rolled up to above the knees, his pale white, hairy legs in a tub of hot water, he added bath salts to the water until it tickled his toes.

Bent forward, his face distorted in a grimace of pain and discomfort, he rubbed his ankles. It seemed as if legions of little devils were sticking sharp needles in his lower extremities. The pain caused an uncomfortable feeling of defeat. He knew the meaning of the pain. It was an old acquaintance. Whenever an investigation was going badly, or was at a dead-end, it came. Whenever he felt himself drifting away from the solution, it came. The farther he was off the track, the worse the pain would be. His feet suffered most. He looked sideways and upward at his wife.

"You want some more hot water?" she asked concerned, unable to alleviate his pain, but willing to help anyway she could. The heavy kettle in her hands steamed.

"Carefully," he nodded. There was fear in his voice. Carefully she added hot water to the tub.

"More?"

He made a negative gesture.

"You don't have to boil me alive," he commented gruffly. "I'm no lobster!"

Mrs. DeKok laughed. She knew the moods of her husband better than he knew them himself. His bad humor was a direct result of his job and had little to do with his feet.

"You haven't solved it yet?" she asked sweetly.

DeKok moved his feet and rubbed them against each other.

"Solved what?" he asked superfluously.

"The murders on the menu."

He shook his head. It was a tired and discouraged gesture. He grumbled:

"At one time the solution of a murder was like a crossword puzzle, now they're cryptograms." He lifted one of his legs and allowed the water to drip from his foot. "In the old days, a criminal wore a black sweater, a black hat and hadn't shaved for several days. Today the criminals wear Saville Row suits and butter wouldn't melt in their mouths."

Still grumbling he accepted a towel. After a while he pulled his other leg out of the water. Mrs. DeKok shook her head in commiseration.

"Hurry up, Jurriaan," she urged, "time to go to work."

"I am out there at all hours of the night, in all kinds of weather," he snorted. "They can just wait for me in the morning. Do them good to practice a little patience."

Mrs. DeKok sighed theatrically.

"Vledder has called several times already. He wonders where you are."

"So, what does he want, the brat?"

Mrs. DeKok removed the tub and looked accusingly at her husband.

"He's anything but a brat," she said. "He's your colleague. He's a hardworking young man and you like him.

He was rather enthusiastic this morning and said something about an important new development."

DeKok growled again, for good measure, lowered his pants' legs and pulled his socks on.

"What sort of development?"

"He didn't say. He said he wanted to go to Maastricht, as soon as possible."

DeKok broke the lace of his left shoe.

"Maas-tricht? Where they have the European Community talk marathons?"

He spoke the name of the town as if it was a four-letter word.

* * *

As usual, Vledder was pounding away on his electric typewriter as DeKok entered the large detective room. The fast fingers of the younger man formed a blur as they danced over the keys. He waited patiently for the old Inspector to lower himself behind his desk.

"You're late this morning."

DeKok leaned backward in his chair, lifted his legs and pointed at his feet.

"I had tired feet. Last night already, but then I was too tired and numb to think about it. I just rolled into bed and slept almost at once. But this morning they were still tired. Therefore I took the time to spoil my reluctant locomotive body parts with a nice, long, hot bath."

Vledder looked concerned.

"And how are you feeling now?"

His question showed a considerable amount of interest. DeKok closed his eyes momentarily, pinched his calf, lowered his legs and declared, solemnly:

143

"It's gone."

Vledder's face cleared up.

"I'm so happy ... a load off my mind."

DeKok looked at him suspiciously. But there was no mockery in the young inspector's tone, or on his face.

"Did you check on the red Mitsubishi?"

Vledder nodded.

"It was, of course, impossible to issue an all-points bulletin. We can't arrest him. I mean, based on what we have so far, there's no way we can charge Teest with anything. Just driving a red Mitsubishi isn't a crime, yet."

DeKok plucked his lower lip.

"But I would like to know where that car winds up. You see, secretly I share Aggie's fear. I wouldn't be at all surprised if something were to go wrong. No, not at all, at all."

"Another killing?'

DeKok nodded thoughtfully.

"Another killing," he repeated somberly.

"And with Bert Teest as the victim?"

DeKok did not answer. It was as if he had not heard the remark. His face was serious.

"And I have no idea how to prevent it. I'm no clair-voyant. If I knew where ... " He stopped in mid sentence. Suddenly he looked thoughtfully at Vledder.

"My wife said something about Maastricht ... what's the matter with Maastricht?"

"That's where we're going," laughed Vledder.

"Maastricht?"

Vledder nodded emphatically.

"That's where we'll find the widow Donkersloot."

DeKok sat up straight with a violent movement.

"What!?"

Again Vledder nodded.

"Yep, in the rest home 'Rest Region' on the South Lane."

16

Vledder guided the new Golf out of the parking lot, across to the Old Bridge Alley and switched the wipers to maximum speed. The nice sunny weather of the last few days had been chased away by the long announced depression from over the North Sea. Amsterdam was again covered by a low, grey blanket of clouds that produced unending streams of heavy rain. On the wide sidewalks of the shopping areas the female attractions were covered in shapeless drapes of plastic, instead of the sensuous, sometimes revealing, clothing of the previous days. Everything seemed more somber. But, according to DeKok this was really Amsterdam and this was the way it should always be. Amsterdam in the rain, he concluded, looked fresh, the asphalt gleamed and the old facades of the stately houses along the canals gained a new luster. He looked aside.

"You have enough fuel?" he asked, worried. "Isn't Maastricht just about as far as you can go from Amsterdam and still remain in Holland?"

"Yes, yes," nodded Vledder. "I checked it. It's almost one hundred and fifty miles and the tank is full."

"I bet you're happy," smiled DeKok. "Within days after getting the new car, you can try her out on a long trip." His tone shifted slightly to mockery, but he did not wait for an answer. He continued: "How did you manage to find the dear widow's address so suddenly? Did she finally check out of the Rotterdam City Register?"

"I had another call from the kid," answered Vledder.

"What kid?"

"The one who wants to be a detective," laughed Vledder.

DeKok's face cleared up.

"Ah, yes, Jan Schouten ... the bookseller's son."

"Uh, uh, after he learned from us that Madame Donkersloot had disappeared, he decided to practice his detective skills. He looked at it as a sort of test ... to see if he had the required qualities to join the force, later. It seems that he spent days around Mill Lane. Apparently he checked door-to-door to see if anybody did know anything about her disappearance. He came up with some cockamamie story that he used to bring her a present on her birthday, or something, and that he would like to continue the tradition."

"Clever boy," laughed DeKok.

"Yes, well, anyway, he finally got hold of an old lady who had just received a postcard from Mrs. Donkersloot. A nice picture of a large house, surrounded by greenery. A window was marked on the third floor."

"And that's how he found her address?"

"No, no, just her name ... Mrs. Donkersloot. But the picture was a photo of the rest home 'Rest Region' in Maastricht."

"Ah, and the mark on the photo indicated her room?"

"Yes, that's what Jan thought. Anyway, that's how he put two and two together. And I believe he's right."

For a while they drove on in silence. The busy traffic on the slick streets took all of Vledder's attention. Finally, after they reached the main highway to the south, the young inspector looked aside and said:

"This time you'll have to put some direct questions to Mrs. Donkersloot. There's no other way. No more pussy-footing."

DeKok acted surprised.

"What do you mean?"

Vledder paused. He looked searchingly at his older colleague. Then, in a suspicious voice, he asked:

"You took the menus with the confessions, didn't you?"

DeKok nodded calmly.

"That's the reason for this briefcase. I don't usually carry that with me, as you know very well."

Vledder gestured vaguely.

"Well, I think it's time, finally, that we find out whether or not the confessions have indeed been written by her husband ... I want to *see* her reaction."

DeKok nodded understanding. Then, apologetically, he said:

"After all, there was no way to predict that she would suddenly disappear. There was simply no opportunity to show her the confessions after that. Perhaps we'll have an opportunity this time ... thanks to a seventeen year old boy."

"Unless she's meanwhile changed base again," growled Vledder.

DeKok pursed his lips. He shook his head. He made an almost visible effort to control his eyebrows. Then he said:

"One doesn't 'change base' that easily, as you put it, from a rest home. Usually one changes 'base' just one more time after that ... to a final resting place."

* * *

Maastricht looked like what it was: the oldest city in the Netherlands, going back to Roman times. South Lane was a beautiful piece of city planning, restful, quiet and full of greenery. Vledder parked the Golf within a partially walled space in front of 'Rest Region". DeKok emerged rumpled from the car. He stretched. There was no doubt that the new Golf was a lot more comfortable than the old Beetle, but any long drive caused a displacement of muscle, bones, arteries and limbs. It took a while before he had everything rearranged to his satisfaction. Then, briefcase under one arm, he shuffled visibly tired after Vledder toward the entrance. 'Rest Region', thought DeKok, was a masterful example of a utilitarian and aesthetic building in beautiful surroundings. It might not be so bad to spend one's last days here, he thought. He wondered if he should perhaps, after all, reserve a place for him and his wife, just in case. But then, with some melancholy, he reminded himself that it would be a while before his retirement.

A friendly young nurse, in starched whites, led them to a comfortable, roomy elevator and the third floor. In front of one of the apartments she knocked quietly on the door. In response to the soft 'yes', she entered. Within minutes she was back and told the inspectors that Madame was ready to receive them. She opened the door wide for the two policemen. Mrs. Donkersloot looked up when they entered. Her mouth, surrounded by a garland of fine wrinkles, was made suddenly beautiful by a gentle smile.

"I was wondering how long it would take you to find me."

It sounded friendly.

DeKok looked at her searchingly. He decided that Mrs. Donkersloot looked very well, indeed. Much better than the last time, when he had met her in the cold, clammy house in Rotterdam. The silver hair was no longer constrained in a severe chignon and the black dress had been replaced by a stylish suit. The old inspector slowly lowered himself in a rattan chair and said:

"I take it you expected us ... one of these days?"

"I knew you had to talk to me again," she nodded.

"Why?"

"My husband's life, his affairs, his business, would have given you a number of reasons."

"Then you do know more about your husband's outside affairs then you were willing to admit in Rotterdam, at the time?" He smiled.

"I didn't want to spoil the memory of my husband," she said with an apologetic gesture. "He's always been a good husband to me ... loving, dedicated, attentive, old-fashioned reliable."

DeKok cocked his head.

"Then what was there to hide?"

"Hendrik was a different man when it came to business." She lowered her head. "In business he was hard, merciless. He had a passion for earning money, for making money, rather. I told him, more than once, that it was a genetic curse. Our early merchants of the 'Golden Age', in the 17th Century, had the same sort of single-mindedness for trade and profits. He was a throwback, I told him. They didn't care how they made their money, slaves, colonization, piracy, it was all the same to them. Hendrik was a lot like that."

DeKok looked at her evenly.

"Did you know that your husband financed drug deals?"

Slowly, reluctantly, Mrs. Donkersloot nodded in confirmation.

"I knew," she answered softly. "I was against it, always. But he would wave my objections aside. He would laugh and say that if he didn't do it, someone else would fill the gap. And why, he would ask, should he let someone else make all the profits, when he could do it so much better himself?"

DeKok smiled sadly.

"I'm familiar with the argument," he said. Then, gesturing vaguely in her direction, he asked: "And his partners in crime were Frederik Ravenstein, Arnold Boning and Bert Teest?"

"You're well informed," she said full of admiration.

DeKok ignored the remark.

"Have you ever met them?"

"A few times," she nodded. "Repulsive types ... as became clear later, abundantly clear."

"When?"

"When Hendrik wanted to stop. Wanted to get out."

"Why? He had come to realize the destructive effects of the drugs he helped distribute?"

She shook her head.

"No, that wasn't my husband's motive. He had no pity at all for the users. He was incapable of pity for them. People, he felt, had a free choice. If they opted for drugs than it was their own responsibility and they had better be prepared for the consequences."

Confused, DeKok looked at her. His eyebrows vibrated slightly.

"Then why did he want to quit?"

"About two years ago," she sighed, "Hendrik went to South-America in response to a request from the syndicate. He was supposed to make new contacts."

"For drug deliveries?"

"Yes, indeed. The current suppliers, according to the syndicate, were reneging on their agreements and prices kept increasing. New suppliers had to be found. Partly because Hendrik spoke fluent Spanish and, of course, because of his business acumen, he was the unanimous choice. He knew the requirements and the possibilities."

"And then?"

"My husband met the drug lords in South America." She moved slightly in her chair, as if steeling herself for a particularly uncomfortable revelation. Then she continued: "He met the drug lords ... fabulously wealthy criminals, who rolled in wanton luxury, extravagant to the point of ridicule. It was such a revolting example of mis-used wealth that it antagonized him. In his heart Hendrik was always a bit of a pure Calvinist. Excesses are destructive, he felt. Despite the fortunes he made, we never lived in luxury, not really. We were comfortable, we loved each other, respected each other, but in a quiet, not a showy manner. Wealth was not to be advertised."

"Is that why he wanted to get out ... because he didn't approve of the lifestyle of the drug lords?"

"That wasn't the only reason." She shook her head, as if to clear her thoughts. "No, perhaps you'll find this hard to believe, or understand, but the fact is, that my husband, merciless, cold, calculating business man, was in reality an extremely social and conscientious man." She stretched her back and blushed shyly. "I plead for him in this way, because I think he deserves it, something better anyway." She remained silent, as if in thought, sighed deeply and continued: "No, he also saw, in South-America, the poverty and misery of the masses. People, not responsible for their own condition, blameless for their own poverty and ignorance ... in my husband's eyes they were guiltless. People who had no choice, no way of improving their lot in life. Unlike the drug users in Europe. People who had made a choice, unlike the poor, ignorant and diseased masses in South-America who were exploited both by the drug lords and by the users. People who were forced to harvest the products that were openly exported by the rich and willingly paid for by the users." She leaned back in her chair. She paused, sighed again and said: "Those are the people my husband decided to help. The exploited, the poor, the down-trodden. That's why he wanted to leave the syndicate. He wanted to return to South-America, He wanted to help, help in person and in a meaningful way. A sort of one-man Peace Corps."

DeKok remained silent and let her words sink in. He had listened carefully and attentively to her pleading, almost an eulogy for her dead husband.

"The other members of the syndicate wanted to prevent him from leaving?" he asked.

"They put pressure on him," she said, slowly shaking her head. "They tried to blackmail him ... they told him that they would inform Narcotics of his activities ... declared themselves ready to turn Crown's witness. In exchange for immunity they would perjure themselves to prove that he was the guiding force and the guilty party. All sort of threats ..."

DeKok's eyebrows finally got the better of him. They seemed to dance off his forehead.

"Why such hate? When he died they had to carry on without him, regardless."

"My husband was no criminal," she said, slowly. She nodded, licked her dry lips, paused, as if in thought, then she said: "I mean, he had no criminal mentality, unlike the others. He was a businessman. They really never liked him.

They tolerated him, needed him, because of his knowledge, his business sense, his financial wizardry. He was a financial genius, you know."

"Jealousy?"

"Perhaps." Again she nodded slowly. "Perhaps ... yes, you could call it that."

DeKok leaned toward her.

"And how did your husband respond to their threats, their opposition?"

"He seemed mostly sad about it. Perhaps more sad then he showed. I also believe that it affected his health. The constant pressure, the threats, the veiled hints, and some less veiled, made him ill ... the fatal heart attack may have been a direct result of that."

"Did he abandon his plans?"

Vehemently Mrs. Donkersloot shook her head.

"Most certainly not!" she cried enthusiastically. "He went back several times. To South-America, I mean. With his own money he started a number of organizations designed to help the poor. He had plans, plans for a self-sustaining village. A village with schools, a hospital, shops, industry ..."

"Didn't he fear repercussions, revenge, from the syndicate?"

"I don't think they knew," she smiled. "I don't think they even suspected. No, they just didn't know ... what he did in South America. As far as they knew, he continued to work for the syndicate. As far as they knew, nothing had changed."

"But the hate remained ... mutual hate?"

"Yes, certainly. Hendrik couldn't stand the internal bickering. Sometimes, after another of those meetings at the *Poort van Eden* he would talk to me about it. Get it off his chest, so to speak. 'They're bastards!' he would curse. He'd regret that he had ever gotten involved with them. He'd carry on so ..."

DeKok stretched his arms in front of him and pressed the tips of his fingers together.

"Did he ever get the idea ...eh, did he ever discuss with you ...eh, did he ever want to get rid of them ... literally?"

Mrs. Donkersloot looked at him. Genuine confusion was clearly visible on her face.

"You ...eh, you mean, you mean ... murder?"

Calmly DeKok nodded.

"Murder!" he repeated in a sinister tone of voice. He picked up the briefcase, pulled the confession of Ravenstein's murder out and handed it to her. He looked at her with concern.

"Please read this."

Mrs. Donkersloot accepted the menu. She took her glasses from a small table next to her chair, put them on and started to read. Almost holding his breath, DeKok looked at her. Not for a moment did his gaze leave her face, while she absorbed the words of the confession. Before she had read the last line, the menu slipped from her powerless hands and fell on the floor. The much wrinkled mouth opened. She looked at DeKok ... a devastated look of total astonishment in her eyes. Then she closed her eyes and slid to the floor. Unconscious.

17

They drove away from 'Rest Region' in Maastricht. Vledder kept his eyes on the road, a rebellious look on his face, and was silent. DeKok had slid down in the seat, without bothering about seat belts and was also silent. The old inspector had a strange feeling of discomfort. His thoughts were all awry. He was mad at himself and could not pinpoint the reason. The hastily summoned doctor of the rest home had arrived within minutes and brought her around within seconds after that, but he had prohibited the inspectors from questioning her further. According to the doctor, in view of the uncertain health of his patient, that would not have been in the best interest of his patient. He refused to allow it and was not prepared to take the responsibility.

But DeKok had so many questions left ... about the false report in connection with the "theft" of her husband's book collection ... her strange behavior regarding her nephew ... had she planned to join her husband in South America ... what did she really know about Ravenstein's murder? The grey sleuth worried whether or not the moment had been right to confront her with the confession ... perhaps it would have been better not to discuss the confession? There had been a reason for his feeling, his instinct, back in

Rotterdam, when he had been reluctant to show her the confession at that time ... he did not know why, then, and he did not know why, now, but the timing had been wrong, in both instances. He felt it. Yet, he had gone ahead, almost expecting her reaction. Vledder looked at him sideways.

"Now what?" he asked, his voice was close to despair.

DeKok pushed himself slightly higher.

"We'll have to wait a few days, at least, before we can present ourselves once more in Maastricht. And we just haven't got that much time. I'm afraid that developments will rapidly overtake us." He looked at his young colleague and then, with a wry grin, said: "At least you can be satisfied. Your question has been answered."

"Eh, ...what do you mean?" Vledder sounded confused.

"You wanted to know for certain," he began with a tired smile and then, after a short pause: "You wanted to be sure that Donkersloot had indeed been the author, that the confessions had been written by him ... I thought that Mrs. Donkersloot's reaction to the menu would have been sufficient answer, even for you."

"It just doesn't help us much." Vledder nodded slowly. His face was somber when he continued: "Why in hell did she have to faint. People don't do that anymore!" He sighed. "We should have brought her around ourselves. We should have kept that doctor out!" His voice was garrulous.

DeKok looked at him accusingly.

"I don't want the responsibility of making medical decisions, especially in the case of an elderly person ... no matter what the supposed justification. I understand her reaction very well ... if you suddenly discover that your husband, in addition to financing drug traffic, also is involved in murder ..." He did not complete the sentence.

"You don't think she knew?"

158

"I don't think so." DeKok shook his head. "No, I don't think so. In any case, she most certainly knew nothing about the confessions. I've felt that from the beginning, from the moment that young Schouten brought us the first confession. For the simple reason that, if she had known, she would never have sold the collection to the elder Schouten in the first place ... thereby risking the chance that her husband's confessions would wind up in the wrong hands."

"It could have been coincidence ..." Vledder shrugged his shoulders. " ... perhaps she knew about the confessions, but didn't know where they were hidden."

"If she had known about the confessions, she would have looked for them." DeKok shook his head. "She would have looked everywhere, I'm sure, and nothing would have left the house unless it was thoroughly searched, perhaps several times. She would have searched until she had found them and then she would have destroyed them. That's obvious, I'd say."

"Perhaps," nodded Vledder vaguely, "but I can't help the feeling that the old widow knew exactly what was going on, she knew exactly what has happened ... I'm sure she also knows the secret of the mysterious confessions. Perhaps more."

"Well, if you're convinced that she knew everything," answered DeKok, irritated, "then you also have to assume that she knew that her husband had written that he was going to kill Arnold Boning in Amsterdam, at the end of Pier 27." He remained silent for a while, as if to heighten the effect of his words. Then he continued: "Then there remains another important question ... before Donkersloot could complete his plans, he died of a heart attack. So, who felt called upon to complete his plans and who is responsible for the killing of Boning according to such a pre-determined and strict scenario?"

* * *

They entered Amsterdam. Traffic was heavy and it was still raining. Vledder gestured at the windshield as he switched on the wipers.

"All day it's dry," he growled, "and the moment you enter this idiotic city it starts to rain." He pointed up. "Do you think they don't like Amsterdam, upstairs?" He snorted contemptuously. "I wouldn't be at all surprised."

DeKok ignored him. The little wheels in his brain were turning at maximum speed. He just knew that the case was rapidly approaching an inevitable dramatic conclusion ... a violent explosion was not far off. He *knew!* It was paralyzing to know that there wasn't a thing he could do about it. He could only wait. He had neither the means, nor the knowledge, to stop the violence.

Vledder parked the Golf in the lot behind the station and they walked around the building toward the front. DeKok carried his briefcase under one arm. In spite of the long drive, he appeared rested and alert. He looked around. The long lines, the droves of sexually deprived, or those who thought they were sexually deprived were forming up and started to stream in the direction of the Red Light District. Dusk was falling, street lights lit up. As they entered the lobby of the ancient police station, Kusters, the desk sergeant, called them over.

"Another gorgeous girl waiting for you, upstairs," he said jovially. Laughing he shook his head. "What do those children want from you?"

"Name?"

Kusters looked at his notes.

"Anna Breitenbach."

DeKok grinned.

"Not exactly a child to put on your lap."

The old inspector turned and, two steps at a time, climbed the stairs to the third floor.

On the bench, outside the large detective room, he discovered sensuous Anna. She wore the same red coat as during her earlier visit. When she noticed DeKok she stood up and brushed a blonde strand away from her eyes. Meanwhile she looked at her watch.

"I've been waiting for more than an hour!" she accused him. "And every minute is precious. I *must* talk to you."

DeKok looked at her carefully. He found her looking pale and her make-up had been carelessly applied. Mascara had smeared around the eyes and there was a trace of lipstick on her teeth. The long, blonde hair was less lustrous, almost dull. He led her into the large detective room and pointed at the chair next to his desk.

DeKok opened the drawer of an old, battered file cabinet and deposited his briefcase in it. After that, without taking off his raincoat, merely shoving his ridiculous little hat further back on his head, he sat down and waved invitingly in her direction.

"Tell me everything."

Anna Breitenbach pressed her lips together.

"Teest," she hissed.

DeKok spread his arms.

"What about Teest?"

"He's telling everybody that I killed my Friedreich and that I'm also responsible for the death of 'Fatman' Boning!"

DeKok eyed her evenly.

"That's not true?"

"Of course not," she reacted vehemently. "NO! I've nothing to do with either of those murders ... nothing at all! It's slander ... nothing but slander! Now that Teest can't get me, he's trying to get his revenge ... starts to spread rumors. He's a real bastard ... a liar! Peter is furious."

DeKok rubbed the back of his nose with his pinky. He looked at her through outspread fingers.

"Peter Valenkamp?"

"Yes."

"Your lover?"

"For a number of years," she nodded.

"Also while 'your' Friedreich was still alive?"

She hung her head.

"My Friedreich was a dear old man, I loved him ... really. A man who liked to pet me ... caress me." She shrugged her shoulders. "But that was all."

"And that wasn't enough for you?" DeKok understood.

"Eventually, no, it wasn't enough."

"Did Teest know about your parallel relationship with both men?"

Anna closed her eyes momentarily.

"Yes," she sighed. "Yes, he knew. Bert used to allude to this, what did you call it? ... this 'parallel' relationship. He said that there was no reason for me to reject him as a lover, that one more, or less, would hardly make a difference to me."

"Not very gallant," grinned DeKok. He shook his head. "Did Peter know about Bert's attempt to seduce you?"

The beautiful woman hid her face in her hands.

"Peter is going to kill him," she sobbed. Her body shook. "He's taken my pistol and he's planning to shoot Teest like a dog." She looked imploringly at DeKok. "He will do it ... he will, really, he will ... he'd finally be rid of the entire *Poort van Eden* bunch."

"Is that what he said?" A slight vibration disturbed DeKok's eyebrows.

Anna sighed deeply. It did interesting things to her bosom.

"You must talk to him ... you must stop him. I don't want to lose him, too ... like Friedreich. Peter can't stand up to Teest. That bastard is always armed. He'll kill Peter!"

Thoughtfully DeKok plucked at his lower lip.

"The pistol you talked about, the one that Valenkamp now has, that pistol ... is it your 9mm FN?"

"Yes."

"Where is the old Sauer? The 7.6mm that used to belong to Ravenstein. What happened to that?"

Surprised Anna looked at him.

"Friedreich used to carry it with him ... always."

DeKok cocked his head at her.

"He also had it with him the night he was murdered?"

She nodded emphatically.

"Also," she repeated, "on the night he was murdered."

* * *

After Anna had left, Vledder looked a question at the DeKok.

"So, what's our next step? We can hardly wait until Valenkamp butchers Teest ... or vice versa. Now that we know, thanks to Anna, that something's up, we'll have to act. There's no other choice."

The old inspector did not answer at once. He seemed undecided. Without moving a muscle he stared in front of him. Then he took his old, battered, much abused hat from his head and threw it across the room.

"Try to get a hold of Fred Prins and Ab Keizer."

Vledder made a helpless gesture.

"They'll be home, by now."

"Call them at home," DeKok said, agitated. "They have to report back on duty, immediately. I want them to go to the *Poort van Eden* and I want them to persuade Valenkamp to give up his weapon ... for all I care they arrest him for unauthorized possession of a firearm."

"But why don't we go ourselves?" Vledder looked confused. "It's going to take those two at least half an hour to get there."

DeKok shook his head.

"We wait here," he said abruptly.

The old inspector rose and began to pace the large room with long, slow steps. It helped to rearrange his thoughts. He half listened as Vledder picked up the phone and contacted first Prins and then Keizer. Many times before, DeKok had been able to call on these two young colleagues. They had never let him down. They were always ready to cooperate, within, or without the regulations. This, he felt, was an emergency, he did not have the time, or, to be honest, the inclination, to go through channels.

Vledder pulled his electric typewriter closer and started to insert a blank report sheet. Suddenly DeKok stopped his pacing. The phone on his desk rang insistently. Vledder reached over and listened. It took but a few seconds. DeKok watched as his young colleague replaced the receiver. They looked at each other.

"Who was it?"

"Constables on patrol."

"And?"

164

"They've just spotted the red Mitsubishi."

"Where?"

"Western part of the harbor grounds."

DeKok looked at him, expectantly.

"Did they manage to stop him?"

Vledder shook his head.

"They couldn't catch up with him. They lost him around the North Sea Way."

With a lightning movement DeKok grabbed his hat from where it had so carelessly been tossed. He ran to the door. His footsteps shook the old building.

Vledder looked after him for several seconds, unable to move. DeKok at speed was a comical sight.

Then he ran after him.

18

Much too fast for the heavy traffic, Vledder manoeuvred the Golf through the narrow streets of Amsterdam, passed behind the Central Station and headed toward the western harbor area. The engine groaned and the tires screeched in the curves.

DeKok looked at his driver.

"A little easier with your new toy, there. The State is not all that generous. This car has to last a long time."

"Well, you started to run," said Vledder, hurt. DeKok nodded.

"The deserted terrain of the western harbor is exactly the type of spot our murderer would choose. At least, it's the type of spot I would have expected him to pick."

"You think Teest is meeting someone?"

"Yes," nodded DeKok. His tone was somber. "Yes, I think dear Aggie Aleph is going to be proved right. Bert wouldn't listen to me and he's going to take matters in his own hands ... take care of his own business ... his own self ... in his own way ... as always." He shook his head. "If Teest hadn't been such a blasted stubborn and arrogant ...eh, person, if he had told us where the meeting was to take place, then we could have set a trap at leisure. We could have caught the murderer and could have prevented a lot of unnecessary bloodshed. Some people always have to know better," he concluded and sighed, long and deep.

Vledder ignored his soliloquy. He drove along the Transformer Way toward the Basis Way, which bisected all the major roads in the extensive harbor terrain.

"How much farther?" he asked.

"You know how extensive the area is," DeKok shrugged. "It'll be like looking for a needle in a haystack. Just keep to the Basis Way. It'll give us a chance to look down all intersecting roads. There'll be hardly any traffic at this time of night."

To DeKok's considerable consternation, Vledder ignored a number of red lights and reached the Basis Way at speed. They passed the complex of the 'Telegraaf' newspaper, standing like a sentinel next to the gateway of the expansive, vast area of the western harbor terrain. To the left, a single spur, rusty brown, ran between knee-high weeds. DeKok felt tension creep upon him. His old heart beat an uncharacteristic rhythm and the tips of his fingers itched. Vledder did not slow down, but raced along the Basis Way as if competing in the Indianapolis 500. There was not a soul in sight along the long, empty road. DeKok peered intensely down the side roads as they flashed by. Suddenly, off to the right of the road, half hidden by a large trailer, they spotted a deserted police cruiser, lights on and doors open. Vledder braked hard and the car slid to a stop within inches of the apparently abandoned cruiser. Only the much despised seat belts kept DeKok from sliding through the windshield. Vledder pulled up and slowly they passed it. About a hundred yards past the cruiser they found a red Mitsubishi, guarded by a solitary constable.

Again, slipping on the wet pavement, Vledder came to a full stop. They got out of the car and walked toward the young constable. With a wide swing of his arm, he pointed into the darkness.

"A shooting," he said, panting. "Perhaps a few minutes ago. We've spotted the Mitsubishi several times. All over the terrain, but he was just too fast for us. We kept losing him." He turned and led them around the car. "The driver is on the other side. We called the Paramedics, but he's probably dead already."

DeKok looked at him. Wondering at the callous tone of so young a person.

"What about the other?"

The constable pointed off into the darkness.

"A little distance that way. My partner is with him. The guy is seriously injured, but he's still alive ... there's still a pulse."

DeKok bent over near the corpse of the man next to the fire-engine red Mitsubishi. He recognized Bert Teest almost at once. A heavy pistol had dropped, close to his right hand.

The grey sleuth flicked his flashlight on and aimed the light at the wide-open eyes. The pupils did not react.

With creaking knees he straightened himself up and walked toward the second constable. With a bored face, the young constable leaned against a steel roll door of one of the many warehouses. The body of a man was at his feet. When he noticed the two inspectors, the constable straightened himself. He almost came to attention. He pointed at the body.

"I think he was shot first, before he returned fire," he said.

"And why is that?" asked DeKok.

The constable thumbed in the direction of the red car.

"The other one was hit in the back ... perhaps while walking back to his car."

DeKok looked at the victim. He was wearing a green trench coat, of a model affected by a number of movie detectives. His legs were slightly spread. Overcoat and suit coat were opened. Two large blood stains marred the white expanse of the shirt, near the belly. DeKok knelt down and looked at the wounds. Vledder bent over behind him. He felt his breath in his neck.

"The nephew ... Donkersloot's nephew ... Waterman ... Evert Waterman," said Vledder.

DeKok nodded to himself. On the pavement, near the victim's armpit he found a small pistol. The old inspector took a ballpoint from his coat pocket and inserted it into the barrel of the weapon. He rose with the pistol in front of him.

Vledder looked at it and swallowed.

"A Sauer 7.6mm."

19

DeKok opened the door of his home and looked at Vledder who was standing on the steps. The young inspector laughed, a bit shyly. A large bunch of red roses hung from his left hand.

"For your wife. The longer I know you ... the more I admire her."

DeKok appreciated the sentiment. Laughing, he stepped aside.

"Come on in."

"The others here yet?"

DeKok nodded.

"Yep, Ab Keizer and Fred Prins are with my wife, and are telling her tall tales."

"How did they do, last night?"

"No problem. Valenkamp hardly resisted. He was like a lamb. He surrendered the pistol at once, without arguments. They confiscated it. Anna never had a permit for the weapon."

"She was there too, I mean, in the *Poort van Eden*?"

"Yes."

They entered the living room together. Mrs. DeKok rose and shook hands with Vledder. Enchanted, she accepted the roses. She waved an invitation to an easy chair.

"Please, sit down," she cried jovially. "My husband was wondering what could have kept you."

"Evert Waterman is dead," he answered sadly. "I was at the station this afternoon and Kusters told me. The Academic Hospital did what they could, but the belly wounds were too severe."

"I know, I was there," nodded DeKok.

"When?"

"Last night. They called me out of bed. He'd asked for me."

"You talked to him?"

"Yes."

"Long?"

"Long enough." DeKok shrugged. He turned his head sideways. Then he continued, softly: "He passed quite peacefully ... much more peaceful than I would have expected." He paused, stroked the back of his hand in front of his eyes and said: "The moment reminded me of Marianne van Buren* She too, died while I sat next to the bed. But I was closer to her death ... I felt genuine sorrow."

"Not this time?"

"Less."

They fell silent. Keizer and Prins also remained quiet. As if the spirit of Waterman had suddenly manifested itself. Definitive. Penetrating. Unmistakable.

Mrs. DeKok broke the silence.

"Please sit down, all of you," she said, irked. "This isn't meant to be a standing buffet, after all."

They took their seats and DeKok lifted the carafe filled with fine Napoleon Cognac which he kept specifically for special occasions. He poured generous measures in the paper-thin, slightly warmed, luxurious snifters and handed them around. He lifted his glass.

"To the end of the syndicate."

Prins did not respond to the toast.

"What syndicate?" he asked.

DeKok smiled.

"The syndicate, headquartered in the *Poort van Eden*, you were there yesterday. You and Keizer don't know the pre-history. But, once upon a time ... not really a fairy tale ... there was a syndicate that busied itself with the financing of drug deals. The four gentlemen that formed the syndicate, used to meet regularly in the *Poort van Eden*, here in Amsterdam. The leader was one, now late, Frederik Ravenstein, of German origin. The financial manipulations were controlled by an acknowledged expert in the field, one, now also late, Hendrik Donkersloot, originally a street urchin from Rotterdam."

Again DeKok raised his glass.

"I raise my glass to him as well, him whom I never met ... never knew ... but his widow pleaded for his life ... for his extraordinary behavior ... with such eloquence, that some part of her love for him, her admiration for him, has affected me."

DeKok took a long swallow from the cognac and placed the glass carefully on a small table next to him.

"Hendrik Peter Donkersloot was absorbed by a passion for making money. He didn't care how he made it ... if necessary with trafficking in drugs. For drug users ... addicts ... he knew no compassion, no pity. According to him ... it was their own choice ... their own responsibility. One does not have to agree with his views ... but that, in itself, is also a choice. Two years ago the syndicate sent him to South

America in order to make new contacts and to develop new sources of supply. During his visit he was struck by the enormous difference of the opulent lifestyles of the drug lords and the abject poverty of the masses. The old heart of the street urchin, the child of the people, was affected and he decided to do something to alleviate the poverty and ignorance of the people in South America. He founded schools, shops, stores and spent almost his entire fortune for the benefit of the people he wanted to help. In order to avoid friction with the syndicate, he kept his charitable work a secret. Even when he was ready to quit the syndicate in order to devote full-time to his activities in South America, he never told them the reason. But the rest of the syndicate could not permit him to withdraw. They needed his financial advice and acumen. Thus Donkersloot continued to work on behalf of the syndicate."

DeKok raised a forefinger in the air.

"Donkersloot had a nephew ... Evert Waterman ... who he considered, more or less, as a son. The nephew was a teacher in Rotterdam, but was also deeply involved with the fate of the homeless in his town. He was a member of an organization that was concerned with the interests of this oft-forgotten group. One day, about a year ago, as it were by accident, the organization was able to obtain a large property, ideal as a sort of receiving station, half-way house and temporary shelter for the disadvantaged. They had a number of contributions and other sources of income, but they were about a hundred thousand short. Nephew Waterman thought he had a solution. He went to his fabulously wealthy uncle Donkersloot and asked him for the missing funds. Donkersloot expressed his regrets, but told him that no funds were available. For the first time he mentioned his charitable work in South America. He advised his nephew to contact Ravenstein, the late Ravenstein, a man who had earned fortunes with the drug trade. He would easily be able to donate the missing hundred thousand."

DeKok shook his head disapprovingly.

"Nephew Waterman did it all wrong. When Ravenstein refused to hand over the necessary funds, Waterman hinted at the fortunes that Ravenstein had made in drugs. It was an expensive mistake. Ravenstein felt threatened and apparently thought that Waterman had blackmail in mind. Ravenstein was a shrewd man, hardened in crime. He told Waterman that he had changed his mind and that he was prepared to hand over the money in a quiet place. No witnesses. He agreed to meet Waterman behind the Wester Tower. Innocently, Waterman went to meet his doom ... or so Ravenstein thought. When he was eye to eye with Ravenstein, he was suddenly confronted with a pistol ... Ravenstein told him that he only knew one way to deal with blackmailers ... and that was death to the blackmailer. Waterman panicked. He grabbed for the pistol. A struggle followed and Waterman was able to take the pistol away from Ravenstein. This did not impress Ravenstein. It didn't matter at all to him, he said. Waterman was a dead man, there were enough hired killers ... Then Evert fired ... three times he pulled the trigger of the old Sauer 7.6mm. Frederik Ravenstein died on the spot, killed by the bullets from his own pistol. Waterman dragged the corpse to the nearby Prince's Canal and lowered the body into the water."

DeKok paused, took another sip of his cognac.

"It was the prelude, the overture, to later events."

Vledder leaned forward.

"All right ... Evert Waterman killed Ravenstein. But ...eh, why would Donkersloot write a confession, as if *he* had done the killing?"

DeKok replaced his glass on the table.

"I'll tell you. Nephew Waterman went to Uncle Donkersloot and confessed the murder of Ravenstein. This set old man Donkersloot to thinking and he formulated a plan ... a plan that would give nephew his hundred thousand, and more, and at the same time, would provide uncle with enough funds to continue, and perhaps expand, his South American activities."

DeKok drained his glass and poured once more, all around. Then he continued:

"He drew a picture of an enormously profitable transaction ... a transaction that could earn them millions ... he advised his partners to entrust him with all possible funds of which they could dispose. This was going to be the big one. The more they invested, the more they stood to gain. As I said, Donkersloot was well-known as a financial genius. Where money was concerned he enjoyed their complete and unqualified trust. Without giving it another thought they handed over their entire fortunes. Before long Donkersloot had all the ill gotten profits in one bank account. He paid one hundred thousand to his nephew for his homeless project and added another hundred thousand for good measure. The balance was moved to South America. He knew, of course, that his duplicity would be discovered, sooner or later. In that case he could look forward to just one reward ... liquidation."

DeKok took a thoughtful sip from his cognac. His audience was spellbound.

"Well, anyway, Donkersloot had taken certain measures. In order to safeguard his own life, he decided that the two remaining members of the syndicate, Arnold Boning and Bert Teest, had to die ... as soon as possible, as soon as possible ... after he had their money in his hands. And, of course, before they could discover what had happened to their money."

He paused. He made a questioning gesture with the carafe. Keizer held out his glass for a refill. DeKok also replenished his own glass.

"He picked his nephew, the forenamed Evert Waterman, as his executioner," he continued. "In exchange for an additional two murders, Waterman was to receive additional funds for his project. He also promised to make sure that Waterman would not be blamed. He prepared confessions ... one confession for the murder of Ravenstein, meanwhile accomplished ... and additional confessions for the two new murders, of Boning and Teest, which were still in the planning stage. He, Donkersloot, figured, that with a small portion of the funds he had so skillfully embezzled from his partners, he could finance some minor plastic surgery and disappear forever in South America with a new identity. If nephew Waterman was ever found out, or accused of the murders, he would be able to produce the confessions written and signed by his uncle. He would be able to prove his innocence beyond the shadow of a doubt and would probably get away with the perfect crime."

Vledder swallowed.

"So, Donkersloot was a criminal genius, as well as a financial genius," he said.

"Yes," nodded DeKok. "But death came unexpectedly. The clever Donkersloot suffered an untimely demise from a heart attack ... strange ... a dual personality ... criminal, selfish ... but full of pity and compassion for people who, through no fault of their own, were living in poverty, want and need."

DeKok remained silent. Thoughtfully he leaned back in his chair. Looked at the ceiling. He was tired ... telling the story ... the explanations ... it had tired him. He drained his glass. Bewildered, Vledder looked at him.

"But why did Waterman continue? After his uncle's death there was no need ... he was no longer obliged to live up to the agreement ... then, why?"

"Nephew Waterman was of a different opinion," sighed DeKok. "He felt he owed it to the memory of his uncle to continue the murders ... to clean up the mess ... to wipe them out ... also, he ...eh, saw a way to raise additional funds. He figured that the remaining members of the syndicate probably had found out about his uncle's swindle. He contacted Boning and told him that he knew about the money and that he knew where the money was hidden. For a certain consideration, he said, he would be glad to enable Boning to recover the stolen funds."

"So that's why Boning was so eager to go to a deserted spot to meet him," grinned Vledder.

DeKok's face became somber.

"I was unable to warn Boning. By the time I received the confession found by young Schouten, it was too late. But Bert Teest was a cautioned man. He was determined not to suffer the same fate as his cohorts ... he fired before Waterman could take proper aim. But his shots were not immediately fatal. As he walked away, Waterman was able to kill him by shooting him in the back."

"I know at least one person who will rejoice in his death," grinned Vledder without joy.

"Anna Breitenbach," agreed DeKok.

"But," said Vledder suddenly, "We should be able to find a confession for the murder of Teest as well. Possibly also in the book collection!"

DeKok nodded.

"And we have to go back, at least once, to 'Rest Region' in Maastricht. I still have a few questions for the widow Donkersloot."

"Me too!" cried Vledder. "For instance, why didn't she give the books to her nephew?"

"I think she thought it better if the confession of her husband were to be found by a third party, somebody neutral. If her nephew had produced it all of a sudden, he would, at the very least, have been subjected to some unwanted scrutiny by the police."

"And she knew there was more than one confession?"

After a little while, DeKok shook his head.

"I don't think so. If she had known, she would have kept the other two, or destroyed them. It isn't likely that she would have guessed that her nephew would continue the killings after the death of her husband."

Vledder laughed.

"Well, anyway, the case is closed and you have all the answers. I don't understand why you want to ask her anymore questions."

"Just to satisfy my own curiosity. To see if my guesses are right. I'd like to be certain."

"Well, don't bother on my account. I'm certain. But, if you want, I'll be happy to drive you to Maastricht. Anytime! But, not to change the subject, don't we have to inform Narcotics?"

DeKok grinned. It was an attractive sight, it was still his best feature.

"They kept their files from us ... we'll send them ours."

The thought seemed to amuse him.

Again he filled the glasses. Conversation became more general, the syndicate became less important.

Mrs. DeKok emerged from the kitchen with selected gourmet items. She made several trips. The men dug in. During private moments DeKok was the first to admit that his long and happy marriage was probably primarily a result of his wife's extraordinary culinary gifts.

* * *

It was rather late when the last guest left. DeKok sank back in his easy chair and poured another glass of his favorite beverage. His wife pushed a low stool closer and nestled closely to him.

"I knew it all along," she said.

"What?"

"It had to be the nephew."

Surprised, DeKok looked at her.

"You knew?" he asked. His tone was unbelieving.

"Yes."

"Why didn't you say so?"

Mrs. DeKok smiled endearingly.

"There was no logical proof, no legal evidence, and besides ... I knew you would solve it on your own."

---

* See: DeKok and the Dancing Death.

About the Author:

Albert Cornelis Baantjer (BAANTJER) is the most widely read author in the Netherlands. In a country with less than 15 million inhabitants he sold, in 1988, his millionth "DeKok" book. Todate more than 35 titles in his "DeKok" series have been written and more than 2.5 million copies have been sold. Baantjer can safely be considered a publishing phenomenon. In addition he has written other fiction and non-fiction and writes a daily column for a Dutch newspaper. It is for his "DeKok" books, however, that he is best known. *Every* year more than 700,000 Dutch people check a "Baantjer/DeKok" out of a library. The Dutch version of the Reader's Digest Condensed Books (called "Best Books" in Holland) has selected a Baantjer/DeKok book five (5) times for inclusion in its series of condensed books.

Baantjer writes about Detective-Inspector DeKok of the Amsterdam Municipal Police (Homicide). Baantjer is himself an ex-inspector of the Amsterdam Police and is able to give his fictional characters the depth and the personality of real characters encountered during his long police career. Many people in Holland sometimes confuse real-life Baantjer with fictional DeKok. The author has never before been translated.

This author is a proven best-seller and the careful, authorized translations of his work, published by New Amsterdam Publishing should fascinate the English speaking world as it has the Dutch reading public.

DeKok and the Somber Nude
Baantjer

The oldest of the four men turned to DeKok: "You're from Homicide?" DeKok nodded. The man wiped the raindrops from his face, bent down and carefully lifted a corner of the canvas. Slowly the head became visible: a severed girl's head. DeKok felt the blood drain from his face. "Is that all you found?" he asked. "A little further," the man answered sadly, "is the rest." Spread out among the dirt and the refuse were the remaining parts of the body: both arms, the long, slender legs, the petite torso. There was no clothing.

First American edition of this European Best-Seller.

ISBN 1 881164 01 2

DeKok and the Dead Harlequin
Baantjer

Murder, double murder, is committed in a well-known Amsterdam hotel. During a nightly conversation with the murderer DeKok tries everything possible to prevent the murderer from giving himself up to the police. Risking the anger of superiors DeKok disappears in order to prevent the perpetrator from being found. But he is found, thanks to a six-year old girl who causes untold misery for her family by refusing to sleep. A respected citizen, head of an important Accounting Office, is deadly serious when he asks for information from the police. He is planning to commit murder. He decides that DeKok, as an expert, is the best possible source to teach him how to commit the perfect crime.

First American edition of this European Best-Seller.

ISBN 1 881164 04 7

DeKok and the Disillusioned Corpse
Baantjer

DeKok watched, flanked by his assistant Vledder, as two men from the coroner's office fished a corpse from the waters of the Brewer's Canal. The deceased was a young man with a sympathetic face. Vledder looked and then remarked: "I don't know, but I have the feeling that this one could cause us a lot of trouble. I don't like that strange wound on his head. He also doesn't seem the type to just walk into the water." Vledder was right. Leon, aka Jacques, or Marcel, was the victim of a crime. The solution poses a lot of riddles.

First American edition of this European Best-Seller.

ISBN 1 881164 06 3

DeKok and the Careful Killer
Baantjer

The corpse of a young woman is found in the narrow, barely lit alley in one of the more disreputable areas of Amsterdam. She is dressed in a chinchilla coat, an expensive, leather purse is found near her right shoulder and it looks as if she died of cramps. The body is twisted and distorted. Again DeKok and his invaluable assistant, Vledder, are involved in a new mystery. There are no clues, no motives and, apparently, no perpetrators. But the young woman has been murdered. *That* is certain. Eventually, of course, DeKok unmasks the careful murderer, but not before the reader has taken a trip through the seamier parts of Amsterdam.

First American edition of this European Best-Seller.

ISBN 1 881164 07 1

DeKok and Murder in Ecstacy
Baantjer

The driver is killed, shot down, during the assault on an armored truck. An especially cowardly act, according to eye witnesses. The robber made a special effort to turn back and to fire two bullets through the head of the victim. Within an hour after the event, DeKok is already in the middle of the investigation. Is it a coincidence that the transport was carrying an unusual large amount, this time? DeKok, like most policemen, does not believe in coincidences. He fears that the affair is less simple than it appears. He *knows* that the hunt for the murderer is just the beginning and the driver is not going to be the only victim in this macabre dance for more than $3 million. He looks at Vledder, his assistant, who is composing the text of the All-Points-Bulletin: "You know, Dick," he says sadly, "money ... money is an invention of the devil. Some are possessed by it."

First American edition of this European Best-Seller.

ISBN 1 881164 16 0

Also available as a major motion picture, directed by Hans Scheepmaker. Ask for it in your Video Store.

Murder in Amsterdam
Baantjer

The two very first "DeKok" stories for the first time in a single volume. In these stories DeKok meets Vledder, his invaluable assistant, for the first time. The book contains two complete novels. In *DeKok and the Sunday Strangler*, DeKok is recalled from his vacation in the provinces and tasked to find the murderer of a prostitute. The young, "scientific" detectives are stumped. A second murder occurs, again on Sunday and under the same circumstances. No sign of a struggle, or any other kind of resistance. Because of a circumstantial meeting, with a "missionary" to the Red Light District, DeKok discovers how the murderer thinks. At the last moment DeKok is able to prevent a third murder. In *DeKok and the Corpse on Christmas Eve*, a patrolling constable notices a corpse floating in the Gentlemen's Canal. Autopsy reveals that she has been strangled and that she was pregnant. "Silent witnesses" from the purse of the murdered girl point to two men who played an important role in her life. The fiancee could not possibly have committed the murder, but who is the second man? In order to preserve his Christmas Holiday, DeKok wants to solve the case quickly.

First American edition of these European Best-Sellers in a single volume.

ISBN 1 881164 00 4

TENERIFE!

by Elsinck

Madrid 1989. The body of a man is found in a derelict hotel room. The body is suspended, by means of chains, from hooks in the ceiling. A gag protrudes from the mouth. He has been tortured to death. Even hardened police officers turn away, nauseated. And this won't be the only murder. Quickly the reader becomes aware of the identity of the perpetrator, but the police are faced with a complete mystery. What are the motives? It looks like revenge, but what do the victims have in common? Why does the perpetrator prefer black leather cuffs, blindfolds and whips? The hunt for the assassin leads the police to seldom frequented places in Spain and Amsterdam, including the little known world of the S&M clubs in Amsterdam's Red Light District. In this spine-tingling thriller the reader follows the hunters, as well as the hunted and Elsinck succeeds in creating near unendurable suspense.

First American edition of this European Best-Seller.

ISBN 1 881164 51 9

From critical reviews of **Tenerife!**:

... A wonderful plot, well written — Strong first effort — Promising debut — A successful first effort. A find! — A well written book, holds promise for the future of this author — A first effort to make dreams come true — A jewel of a thriller! — An excellent book, gripping, suspenseful and extremely well written ...

MURDER BY FAX

by Elsinck

Elsinck's second effort consists entirely of a series of Fax copies. An important businessman receives a fax from an organization calling itself "The Radical People's Front for Africa". It demands a contribution of $5 million to aid the struggle of the black population in South Africa. The reader follows the alleged motives and criminal goals of the so-called organization via a series of approximately 200 fax messages between various companies, police departments and other persons. All communication is by Fax and it will lead, eventually, to kidnapping and murder. Because of the unique structure, the book's tension is maintained from the first to the last fax. The reader also experiences the vicarious thrill of "reading someone else's mail". After his successful first book, *Tenerife!*, Elsinck now builds an engrossing and frightening picture of the uses and mis-uses of modern communication methods.

First American edition of this European Best-Seller.

ISBN 1 881164 52 7

From critical reviews of **Murder by Fax**:

... Riveting — Sustains tension and is totally believable — An original idea, well executed — Unorthodox — Engrossing and frightening — Well conceived, written and executed — Elsinck sustains his reputation as a major new writer of thrillers ...

About Elsinck:

Henk Elsink (ELSINCK) is a new star on the Dutch detective-thriller scene. His first book, "Tenerife!", received rave press reviews in the Netherlands. Among them: "A wonderful plot, well written." (De Volkskrant), "A successful first effort. A find!" (Het Parool) and "A jewel!" (Brabants Dagblad).

After a successful career as a stand-up comic and cabaretier, Elsinck retired as a star of radio, TV, stage and film and started to devote his time to the writing of books. He divides his time between Palma de Mallorca (Spain), Turkey and the Netherlands. He has written three books and a fourth is in progress.

Elsinck's books are as far-ranging as their author. His stories reach from Spain to Amsterdam, from Brunei to South America and from Italy to California. His books are genuine thrillers that will keep readers glued to the edge of their seats.

The author is a proven best-seller and the careful, authorized translations of his work, published by New Amsterdam Publishing should fascinate the English speaking world as it has the European reading public.